Dear Disappeared Dad

Dear Disappeared Dad

Written by

Bette Millat

proving
press

Book design and production by
Columbus Publishing Lab
www.columbuspublishinglab.com

Paperback ISBN: 978-1-63337-352-5
E-book ISBN: 978-1-63337-354-9

Printed in the United States of America

To all of my amazing grandchildren.
Follow your dreams, wherever they lead

Chapter One

I'M WRITING A LETTER TO MY DAD.

Dear disappeared, deadbeat dad,

You've missed out on most of my life. Do you even care? I've been waiting for you to come back, and I'm losing hope.

Signed: Your angry daughter,

Amber

Suddenly, my alarm jolts me awake. Turns out it was just a dream, another type of a lie.

Lately, my life has turned into a nonstop waiting game, because my whole existence has become one humongous lie, thanks to my mother.

I'm fumbling to hit the snooze button, but it starts up again all too soon. With a groan, I get up for school and grunt as my feet hit the cold linoleum floor. My stomach rumbles, not just because I'm hungry, but because I found her to be so completely untrustworthy that I couldn't make myself eat dinner last night. Shivering, I stumble to the tiny downstairs bathroom, because she's hogging the only one with a shower and tub.

We take turns to be fair. How ironic is that, knowing now that she is not the model of fairness I thought she was. I stomp over and crank up the heat, because she drops it to an ice-popsicle sixty-five degrees nightly to save money, making me burrow under two thin blankets and a thankfully heavier bedspread.

Thumping back upstairs, I hear her finally come out, and we pass each other in the narrow hall without a word. We haven't spoken since last night, which was more yelling on her part than talking. She found me reading her diary a few days ago, which is what her generation calls their writing journals, because I had to find out the truth.

After grabbing my usual Eggos and juice, I'll wait for the school bus and freeze while I'm at it, since it's crazy cold here in central Ohio for just after Thanksgiving. On top of that, the bus driver never has a set time I can count on. Later, Mom will get home from work and cook dinner, because we take turns there too. Sometimes on Fridays, if I cook, she'll take my BFF (best friend forever), Chloe Maddox, and me to the mall or the movies. Chloe and I have been best friends since kindergarten.

I'm waiting to learn to drive, which can't happen soon enough for me. I'm waiting for the perfect guy in a starry, distant future. I'm especially waiting for my father, who disappeared when I was four. I thought he was dead, till I found out differently when I read Mom's diary.

I finish my Eggos and juice and grab my coat. I slam the door on the way out and trudge down the block to wait for the bus in the freezing cold, like I said. A few other kids also are waiting for the bus, stomping their feet to stay warm. The bus finally arrives and we are carted off to jail, I mean school.

IN SCHOOL, first period class creeps by. I feel so bored, like part of the furniture. I also know I will be called down soon to meet with the guidance counselor, Mom joining us to talk about the last fight I had with the "mean girls."

Currently, I'm sitting and watching the clock, stuck in the guidance counselor's office with my mom, wondering if she'll tell the truth about my dad. I've got this allergic itchiness that activates itself in the presence of liars. It's really fired up now, because she's the biggest liar I know. For the second time this month, she's left work early to show up here, because of stuff happening in school. Neither of us feels any warm, fuzzy connections to each other, any more than the last time they dragged me down here.

I wiggle around, waiting for my turn to talk, listening as Mrs. Savage explains why I should be seeing a family counselor. She clasps her long, bony fingers together and leans forward to look Mom in the eye and pastes what passes for a smile on her face.

"It's my firm belief that Amber will benefit from speaking with a good family counselor." She rambles on about my low grades, loss of interest in school, not to mention my two fights in one month, which has led to this meeting and an all-week in-school suspension.

Mrs. Savage shoves a list of counselors certified to help "troubled youth," as she puts it, across the table and taps on a name that's been circled in bold black marker.

"I would like to recommend Dr. Jenkins, who's had over twenty-five years of experience working with young people, especially ones from single-parent homes, Mrs. Wilcox." I notice my mother start squirming in her seat at that comment. "Of course you're free to choose your own professional."

She smiles encouragingly at Mom. "We don't want fighting with others to become a pattern, now do we?" She sits back in her plush leather chair, swiveling it from side to side, her fingertips forming a big A shape. She gives my mother a self-satisfied smirk, waiting for her reply.

Newsflash, people: it has nothing to do with the fact that I'm fourteen and trying to "find" myself, or my mother's marital status. It has everything to do with my mom's story about what happened to my dad, and the two mean girls who like to bully anyone not in their crowd.

Now they're discussing different groups in school that may be influencing me. I feel sweat beading up under my bangs and around my neck. Just because I smacked down a couple of "mean girls" when Chloe wasn't there to hold me back doesn't prove I have "an uncontrollable temper." They were spreading

4

rumors about how my dad is in jail for being connected to the mob. Idiots! This is Columbus, Ohio, not some TV show featuring the Mafia.

I shudder to think that I once called them friends back in grade school. They were jealous of how tight Chloe and I have always been, because we were all friends in kindergarten. They started picking on me, because I have no dad, and now they are over the top with their nastiness.

Fast facts: nobody, including me, knows my dad, except for my mom. She said he died a war hero in Afghanistan when I was four. That was what I always told anybody who was nosy enough to ask. And I am just being myself: plain old Amber May Wilcox, not part of any goth, punk, or even preppie group that they continue to speculate about, talking over me like I'm not even here. This puts me in the bizarre position of supposedly being influenced by a group I am not in and sticking up for a father I can barely remember. I've only seen him in a couple of slightly out of focus, dog-eared pictures. He was wearing civilian clothes, instead of a military uniform. That should have been clue number one.

Now, Mrs. Savage is bringing up my so-called "anger management problems." Crap. Why is it so hot in here? I'm feeling dizzy. They're not giving me a chance to talk. This cramped little office is closing in on me. Mom and Mrs. Know-It-All Savage are blurring out, but not before I see my mom's expression: a mixture of horror and guilt. Then everything goes black.

Chapter Two

OKAY, THREE DAYS later I'm in this Dr. Jenkins's office. It's some hole-in-the-wall place, and it literally stinks like sweaty old sneakers and unwashed gym socks. I sit and twirl a hunk of my wavy brown hair around my fingers and stare in fascination at his shiny bald head, one wisp of white hair sticking straight up like it is standing at attention. He's telling me he thinks I have been under stress, which accounts for me passing out. Duh! The doctor already checked me out and said nothing was physically wrong. He said I probably hyperventilated and should take deep breaths to calm down. Anyhow, Dr. Jenkins has these thick glasses that make his eyes look bug-like. I can't take this guy seriously.

"Why do you think you are having problems in school, and losing your temper? Your mother tells me you've been suspended for a week because you've been in two fights in one month." Then he grins like that's funny.

Admittedly, I'm only 5'1", but I can hold my own in a fight, just ask anybody. I glare at him, refusing to talk. He seems happy asking dumb questions and then answering them, so I busy myself admiring my newly sculpted nails. I had to practically get down on my knees and beg for them, with Mom finally giving in while moaning on about the cost.

"Perhaps you feel depressed that your father died when you were just four." He's finally scored a hit.

"That's false," I snap, unable to stop myself. "Maybe you should check my mom for signs of depression. She sits drinking wine at night, has crying fits, and lies to me about my dad. I read her dumb diary, and I know for a fact he's not dead, and he's certainly no war hero. She made all that up. He just up and left us, and she has no idea what happened to him."

Dr. Jenkins looks more shocked that I'd broken into my mom's personal journal, instead of realizing she had started this whole thing. Just like a grown-up.

"It's time to have your mother join us," he says decidedly, and leans into his speakerphone, talking to his secretary.

I yell, "Don't I get to say anything about this?" Sweat is beading under my bangs again in under ten seconds. My heart starts racing, which it's done a lot of recently.

"I don't want her in here throwing hissy fits and yelling at me. You told me I could talk to you confidentially." I try to take a deep breath but end up holding it instead of letting it out slowly, like the doctor suggested.

"You need to see how your actions affect others, Amber, and also to listen to her reasons for withholding information

7

about your father." He pushes a button on his phone. There's a knock on the door. His secretary pops her head in, my mom peeking out from behind her. She tries to smile at me as she slides into the seat next to me, but I refuse to even glance her way.

"Why don't you share what we were just talking about with your mother, Amber?" Dr. Jenkins says smoothly.

"You do it," I snap, "since you're like the puppet master here."

Mom looks shocked.

Unperturbed, Dr. Jenkins scribbles something down and proceeds to tell her everything I just said. She starts crying. I should feel satisfied, but I feel sick to my stomach instead.

"Why did you lie to me like that?" I yell. "I won't believe a thing you say ever again." I'm hyperventilating and feeling dizzy again. I force myself to take deep breaths, fighting for control. It's working now, but it didn't when I was dealing with my tormentors. I had already figured out I should breathe slowly or count to ten, but I just didn't care, considering what those two had done. I didn't stop either, until the teacher pulled us apart. I had scratches on my face, plus a couple of strands of hair were yanked out. The worst thing was a torn earlobe, due to my pierced earring being ripped out. But each time, they each received a fat lip and a black eye to match.

"I still can't believe you did that! I would never do something like that to you," Mom wails.

"You are so low tech," I sneer, and turn away, not wanting her to see that I feel guilty. "Besides, all you do these days is cry, drink wine and write in your stupid diary at night. So, I decided to see what was up. You hide stuff from me just as much as you say I do to you. You're a total hypocrite. No wonder that guy Luke you were dating disappeared on you." Her look turns furious, and then she leans over and slaps me. Like mother, like daughter, I guess. Dr. Jenkins looks shocked; he knows he's losing control over the situation.

"Well, here's how her actions affect me." I rub my throbbing cheek, glaring at him, incensed that adults always think everything has to be the kid's fault.

"Ah, ladies, I must insist we try to remain calm." His voice sounds shaky. "You each feel betrayed by the other," he says, sending an apologetic look my way, "but Mrs. Wilcox, really, you are the adult here. I will tolerate no violence. If that ever happens again, I am duty bound to report it. Now please stay calm and tell us why you felt it was necessary to create some less than truthful story about your husband."

We're finally getting somewhere. I continue rubbing my reddened cheek, still feeling mad.

"I had to, can't you see?" She's wearing a pleading look on her face as she glances from him to me, hoping one of us understands. "I had to try to build a good picture of a loving father, so that she would think men were okay to have in her life later on. I didn't want her having the same bad feelings I had about my father. He was an angry, unhappy man. We never did reconcile, and my own mother never forgave me for that. I decided nothing was worth the terrible guilty feelings I knew she would have later in life. All kids feel like a divorce is their fault. You know that's true, Doctor. I was just trying to protect my child from all that misery."

She turns directly to me and says, "I am so sorry, sweetie, about this horrible mess. I started lying, and over time it just snowballed until I couldn't stop. I was so upset after Luke left, and you were asking for more and more information about your dad that I lost my way for a while. I feel awful, sweetie."

She dissolves into tears again, which makes me do the same. She is my mom after all. And the heck with that loser, Luke; I never liked him anyway. I feel the so-called waterproof eyeliner I'm wearing streaking all over. My head is on her shoulder and now she's hugging me, even harder than she'd slapped me.

"Well," says Dr. Jenkins in a relieved and upbeat tone, "we certainly have made good progress for our first session. Now that this is all out in the open, we can work on mending broken fences, so to speak, eh? My receptionist will set a time for next week." He's smiling but looking at his watch with obvious relief.

I feel an indignant scowl darken my face. "Why do I have to come back? This is between my mom and me. I don't need any more counseling." I'm thinking, if this ever gets spread around school—and it probably will, since Mrs. Savage's secretary is Mean Girl Kelly's mom, who has a big mouth like her snotty kid—I will never live down the fact I've been to a shrink.

I don't have a ton of friends in my corner either, since I expect a lot from them, including something called loyalty. I used to like my teachers and get pretty good grades, before I thought they were swapping stories about my sudden temper tantrums to each other. I felt so furious at my lying mother that I started losing it at school and not studying for tests. Plus, I still hear words like *nerd* and *loser* from Casey and Kelly ringing in my ears day after day; yet another good reason why I blew up and gave them both fat lips. Watch out for the little nerd with a fast right hook, witches!

"Well, there's the matter of your panic attacks, for one, and yes, that's what I think is happening here," he says, cutting off any possible argument, "plus your anger management issues. Also, you are a teenager, working on your identity issues."

If I hear that line one more time I'm going to barf! I roll my eyes as he drones on. Dr. Jenkins switches his attention to Mom as I ignore him.

"Clearly, Amber could benefit from continued sessions, Mrs. Wilcox, until at least some of these issues are resolved." Mom nods in agreement, making me mad at her again. My protests turn loud, but to no effect. I am stuck with Mr. Bug Eyes for who knows how long to come.

Chapter Three

MY IN-SCHOOL suspension is over and I am sitting in American History. We're studying the Civil War. Terrific! I've got my own kind of war going on at school, and more to come when I get home. This is the worst class, with both bullies in it and no Chloe to keep a lid on things.

Casey is whispering away to Kelly, while staring at me non-stop. They're both still sporting rainbow colors around their eyes, courtesy of yours truly. Kelly, who sits off to one side of me, is sending me an If-Looks-Could-Kill glare and mouthing a nasty word. I return the compliment and flip her off for good measure.

Uh-oh, Mrs. Blake just saw that.

"Amber, will you kindly face front and try to listen, since you have missed so much class time?"

Malicious laughter erupts from behind me, so I have to defend myself. "Mrs. Blake, I did well on my makeup test, and I also have all the classwork up to date."

"That's wonderful, but I have yet to receive any makeup homework which is worth a third of your grade, plus interims are only two weeks away. So can you please focus and allow me to continue teaching, without wasting any more class time?"

I slump in my seat feeling defeated and listen to the chorus of snickers rippling through the room. Mrs. Blake continues her lesson of how history is the story of families, all living way back in the day. My mom says to stay in the moment; the past is over, it can't be changed, so forget it. Point taken, I suppose, except when you try to rewrite history like she has. I wonder what Mrs. Blake would say to that approach.

When I asked Mom for the actual truth about my dad, she said he was a jazz trombonist playing in noisy, smoke-filled bars. They were just too young and he couldn't support a family after I was born. So they moved in with my grandparents. She said my grandfather really hated that she'd been so "irresponsible." Everybody fought all the time and little me cried constantly, so my parents separated, attended marriage counseling, and tried again. Nothing worked, so they got divorced.

Tragedy struck soon after, when her parents were run off the road by a double hitched semi and were killed. They had left everything to her, which turned out to be hardly anything, since Grandpa had lost a lot of his retirement money in the stock market because of some famous Ponzi scheme. This was probably part of the reason why he was so grouchy all the time.

Mom sold her childhood home and went back to school. She's now an office manager for a nursing home. Still, we are just scraping by, because she claims she can't locate my father to get any child support. Also, since my paternal grandparents passed away when I was two, she can't ask for their help to track him down either.

Both my parents are only children, so we have that in common, I guess. But now, whether she likes it or not, I want to find my dad and get to know him. This idea took hold when I had that dream of him. He's got a lot of explaining to do, and I'm determined to make him pay up, at the very least. What kind of dad disappears on his kid?

I've been listening with one ear as Mrs. Blake drones on about the importance of family trees. Did she mean the rich families that lived on those grand Southern plantations? They fought to continue their way of life, including slavery, for their descendants, so their grandkids and great-grandchildren etc., could be born with silver spoons in their mouths, I suppose.

Both the North and South had lots of branches of their family trees snapped off permanently, now didn't they? And what about the poor slave families that were torn apart? We all know about Harriet Tubman saving her people from that evil. Mrs. Blake's explanation makes me start waving my hand around until she sees me and breaks off her monologue.

"What is it now, Amber?"

I should have known better than to sound interested, but I am annoyed by the whole idea of people getting rich from the unpaid labor of the less fortunate. Even though it happened over one hundred and fifty years ago, slavery still exists today, except now they call it human trafficking. Plus, some rich people are still taking advantage of poorer immigrants right here in our country, paying them peanuts because many are considered illegal and don't dare ask for fair wages.

So I say, "Plantation owners and their families were no worse off than the slaves, whose families were torn apart all the time, and auctioned off, never to see their loved ones again, right?" I continue my argument in spite of the bored looks coming from some kids and my teacher's surprised demeanor. "What about their modern-day descendants? How can they even trace their family trees, when their ancestors got split up and sold off?"

Mrs. Blake presses her mouth into a thin line. She now seems embarrassed, because a couple of African American kids look uncomfortable. I hear groaning noises from the "Gruesome Twosome" behind me.

"Yes, it is all very sad, Amber, which is why we have to learn from our history so we can make progress. We have learned there is only one race—the human race—and we are all a part of it."

She seems satisfied with her answer, but that really didn't start happening until Martin Luther King and Rosa Parks stood up for minority rights, way after the Civil War, like a hundred years later. Hello! On top of that, lots of today's families aren't so perfectly put together either. For some reason, I feel my throat tighten up; now my eyes are watering, so I tell myself not to cry. I hide behind my book until class is over.

The bell rings at last, and I am racing past both Casey and Kelly, but not fast enough. Casey smashes her loaded binder and textbooks into my shoulder, "on accident, so sorry" she says with a crocodile smile, while Kelly sneers openly.

"Thanks for sharing another one of your pathetic life moments with the class, Amber."

"Have you checked out your own loser self in the mirror lately?" I taunt back, and I would say more, but there's no opportunity because we are being pushed by the surge of kids behind us trying to break through the bottleneck of students still stuck in the doorway. We have over thirty kids in a class due to overcrowding and underfunding in the school district.

I'm heading off to lunch where I'll get to talk things over with Chloe, who keeps me sane in this stressful school environment. Slamming my binder into my locker, I grab my lunch sack and shove my way down to the cafeteria. She's already there, not a blond hair out of place, trendy clothes, as usual, spreading her lunch out with precision. She's the total opposite of me, yet somehow we hardly ever disagree. Even Kelly and Casey look up to her, wishing she were still friends with them. One other friend usually sits with us too, but I see Rachel's absent today.

"So, how'd it go with 'Miss Devious and Miss Deception' today?" She has to talk pretty loud over the din of the sixth period lunch crowd, while picking away at her homemade hummus and avocado sandwich, in contrast to my boring PB&J.

Believe me, Chloe wouldn't be caught dead eating the school lunches, loaded as they are with fat and cholesterol. She works out and doesn't possess an ounce of fat on her. I hope someday her healthy eating habits will rub off on me, but I'm not overweight yet, and Mom sure can't afford a gym membership for us like Chloe's family has. Anyway, lately, all I want to eat are chips and Kit Kats. I automatically duck as Calvin, a kid I used to be friends with, tosses a bag of Fritos down to someone at the end of our table. Talk about feeding time at the zoo!

"The usual," I say with a shrug. "How's your day going?"

"Same here," she says, hunting for her napkin. "I've got a ton of homework already, and there's that science test on Monday. There's choir practice after school tonight for the Winter Fest concert next month." I nod and reach for a Kit Kat, which makes her wrinkle her nose at me. "If you keep eating that junk you'll be a walking garbage can. I don't get how your face always stays so clear."

Now I am grinning. "I will take that as a compliment, 'cause I need every one I can get these days. Seriously, though, I am thinking about finding my dad."

Chloe's always up to speed about everything that's happening, like with my mom's lies and even Dr. Jenkins too. She knows I read Mom's journal and found out my dad is still alive, but I hadn't dropped this bombshell yet. Her perfectly plucked eyebrows shoot straight up at my announcement.

"What in the world are you talking about? Where would you even start looking?"

"Well, I have this crazy idea. I might post some information about him on the internet, along with a drawing, which I can do from the only two pictures I have, but showing him much older, of course. I need to find out about him and try to connect. He's my dad, for crying out loud."

She looks amazed but thoughtful. "It's pretty wild, but it just might work. Every once in a while you hear about somebody finding lost relatives through the internet. There was a homeless guy I heard about on YouTube recently who spoke in this cool-sounding radio announcer voice while begging for money. Somebody recorded him on their iPhone and sent it to one of the news channels. Anyway, before you know it, he was reunited with his family. But you'd need to be careful. You don't want some pervert tracking you down or something."

Chloe looks worried but still thoughtful and then continues. "Still, you could put up a drawing of what he might look like now. If you make a website where people could reach you using a contact page, maybe you could weed out the weirdos." Her worried look changes into an optimistic one. "You're such a good artist, Amber. I can picture this happening and would love to help you set it up."

I am grinning from ear to ear. "I knew I could count on you! With what you know about computers, you should be a web designer or maybe even create a whole new social network. I could be your partner and we'd be fantastically rich!"

Chloe cracks up. "You're so hilarious, Amber. Nothing like thinking big, I guess." She sighs. Lunch is over already. Reality catches up to us. One more class to go.

"Let's hang out sometime this weekend," I call over my shoulder. "I can't wait to get this up and running." She waves as she weaves her way through the crowd to her language arts class. Meanwhile, math and quadratic equations await me down the hall.

Chapter Four

BOUNCING AROUND on the bus ride home for thirty minutes listening to my second-best friend, Lucie, talking about her manga characters just doesn't do it for me. Lucie is cool, but let's face it, she's not like Chloe. I can only take Lucie in small doses. We have art class together and ride the bus to school and back, but that's about the extent of our friendship. She said she was almost afraid to sit next to me after I had mixed it up with the "mean girls." She thinks I need to learn to "peace out" more. Making peace with those two is definitely last on my bucket list.

Suddenly, Calvin, who is sitting behind us, pops his head up and shoves it in between us, just as Lucie's showing me her latest manga how-to book. Calvin and I used to be pals in fifth grade, hanging out all the time, until he joined a baseball team at age eleven and, quote, "had no time left over for 'dumb girls' who don't know one end of a bat from the other." He hurt me back then, and he hurt me again more recently when he acted like he cared about me, only to change his mind yet again. He now makes mean comments and cuts me down in front of his friends to get them to laugh at his wisecracks.

Yeah, that and a million other comments from kids through the years about my being so short and having no dad. I toughened up and started talking trash when they teased me about how Mom and I are poor and live in a non-luxury apartment where rents are not sky high.

So, I can't afford designer clothes or go to a tanning salon, big deal. The outside isn't as important as what is on the inside, or so I've been told.

And now, Calvin is at it again. "Hey, Wilcox, I heard about your cool catfights from my buddies here." He's acting all tough for his buddies to see he hates me.

"Next time wait until we can be there to watch you in action." He and his moron pals split their guts laughing. Why did I ever think this kid was cool? Still, I keep hoping he might come to his senses some day so we can actually be friends again.

"Keep it up, Calvin, and I might have to use your ugly face for a demonstration," I warn him. My cheeks are burning as he and his friends continue to snicker at my expense.

"I'd like to see you try." His eyes start narrowing into slits. So, I have to oblige him.

As soon as I punch him, Lucie starts shrieking, "Amber, stop, you're crazy. O-M-G!" Calvin's nose starts spurting blood. He's bellowing like a rampaging elephant.

"I'm not supposed to hit girls, but I'm making an exception in your case." He's up and swinging, but I block him easily while landing a tooth-jarring crack to his jaw. His eyes turn glassy as his friends yank him back into his seat. The bus driver pulls over and is slinging her hefty body down the aisle toward us.

"Amber Wilcox, you are officially off this bus for the rest of the year!" she sputters. "The principal will be calling your mother to confirm this." Her overgrown eyebrows are squashing together like a rainforest jungle, and she's turning weird colors.

Oops, I guess I stepped in it again, and by the look on Lucie's face, I lost another friend too. Maybe Dr. Jenkins has a point about me needing anger management help after all.

Chapter Five

MR. WAYNE, ALIAS the "Never-Listens-To-My-Side-Of-The-Story" principal, called my mom at work. She must have taken off early again because she bursts into my room without any regard for my privacy. I'm in the middle of texting Chloe while listening to my iPod.

"Hand over your cell phone," she screeches. "You are so grounded, maybe forever. I can't believe you got into another fight. Are you trying to get yourself expelled? Do you want me to lose my job and have both of us living in some homeless shelter? That's what will happen if I have to leave work one more time to keep you out of trouble. Then you won't have that new laptop you insisted you needed for school, or glitzy new nails, or even enough food on the table!" My earbuds are in and my music's cranked up, playing Beyoncé, but she's no match for my mom's voice hitting some unbelievably high notes of her own.

"Thanks to your latest bad choice, I'll have to get us up even earlier in order to get you to school before work, if they ever let you go back, that is! You'll have to find something to do at school afterward until I can pick you up." She pauses to suck in air.

"Mother, you seriously need to stop breaking my eardrums," I tell her, calmly shutting off my tunes. "You're the one who's always telling me to stick up for myself. I am just following your parental advice. And there's no way I can stay after school until five o'clock. I would have to be in some club or in sports. You know that."

She collapses on the edge of my bed, breathing hard like she's just run a marathon, and puts her hands up to her face. "Things just can't continue on like this, Amber. I'm calling Dr. Jenkins for an emergency meeting on Saturday." Tears are dripping through her fingers as she mumbles something about being a bad mother. Talk about extremes! I hate it when she gets like this. I chew on my bottom lip, confused about how to respond to her mood swings.

I wish I could tell her how I really feel about everything: I realize I'm complicating her life; I'm feeling like my own is out of control; and now I want to find my dad. But the words just won't come out.

Instead, I find myself saying, "Can you please just get out and leave me alone?"

She wipes her eyes and stares at me for what seems forever, then holds out her hand for my cell phone and says, "Fine. Have it your way." The door slams behind her, my mumbled "whatever" left unheard.

Chapter Six

MOM WAS SO mad when she left my room with my phone in hand that she forgot about this thing called "messaging" on my laptop. I left word for Chloe on her Facebook messages and told her not to bother trying to call me on my cell for a while, until my maniac mother, as I am now referring to her, manages to get back to normal.

I worry about her sometimes, about her own coping skills in general. I mean, she's great with her office software, and using her "hands free" cell phone holder to comply with the new no-texting-while-driving law, but I was the one showing her how to set up her profile and get started with her online dating! We actually had a fun time selecting the perfect picture for her to post. I felt like we were good friends then, before things got so messed up. I know being a single parent is rough on her; heck, it took me six months of constant encouragement to get her to even consider online options and then look what she went through. Obviously, they don't screen out the freaks thoroughly enough. Also, she sure doesn't get the fact that her "little girl" is growing up. Well, that's a no-brainer; parents never see that coming, do they?

I see a reply come in from Chloe. Nonjudgmental as always, she says she'll get in touch soon, and for me to start the drawing of my dad. I have the whole weekend to do that now, with plenty of study time for my science test on the phases of the moon. No worries there, because I can visualize their positions in my head. Being good at art does have certain advantages.

But first, I need to see what Mom is up to, since the pictures of my dad are in a shoebox up on the top shelf of her bedroom closet. I know she keeps them in there, because I saw her drag the box out late at night when she thought I was asleep. I heard her say his name and start crying. That's when I decided I had to break into her diary. Cracking my door open slowly because it's squeaky, I hear her banging the pots and pans around that she forgot to clean last night after I made dinner. Fair is fair; we alternate on cleanup duty as well.

I hop across the tiny hallway to her room and grab a chair to stand on. She thinks she's hiding the box by stashing it way back behind some junk piled way up high. The mess almost topples over as I'm reaching past it, because I'm on my tiptoes and way off balance. Finally, I wrestle the box free, put the chair back and sneak back to my room. It's gotten quiet downstairs, and I almost panic that her "Mom radar" somehow knows what I'm up to, until I hear her call up to me to come downstairs and set the table.

"In a minute," I yell back. I wrestle with figuring out the very old scanner in her bedroom, and I finally get a couple of pictures uploaded to my laptop. I will have to transfer them to a thumb drive, along with everything I write about him, for back-up. That way she can never stumble across them if she comes in unannounced. It would have been so much easier just to take pictures of them on my phone, but since it's been confiscated for who-knows how long, I have to do things the hard way.

While I'm debating if I have time to get the original pictures back, I hear her cell phone's goofy ringtone. It's a song from *The Sound of Music*. I liked that movie when I was little, until I saw how she'd cry nonstop over Maria finding true love. Those waterworks ruined it for me after that.

She takes a couple of calls and keeps talking in hushed tones as if hoping I can't hear. Luckily for me, I have just enough time to put the pictures back where I found them and hustle on downstairs to help out.

Chapter Seven

"DR. JENKINS SAYS he can see us tomorrow at two o'clock, Amber, and don't bother rolling your eyes at me or complaining about it."

"I'm not," I say, to placate her, and then start pulling clean plates out of the dishwasher to hand her while she stirs up beef stew from the crock-pot. We have a lot of one-dish meals like this, which we plan together when we aren't mad at each other. I find I'm hungry, in spite of feeling furious over getting kicked off the bus for the rest of the year.

I heard her agree to the school officials' demand to meet with "the team" for another conference with Mom and me. She got the call right after she stormed out of my room and stomped downstairs to the kitchen.

She'd talked softly then too, but I could still hear the conversation. I feel my jaw tightening up just thinking about the injustice of it all. Even Kelly and Casey only got lunch detentions for two days compared to my three-day stay in the "time out" room.

Right after that one, she took a call from Calvin's mother. I could hear them talking about how we had once been real good friends and wondering what had happened to make us dislike each other so much. Next, they were mutually apologizing for their kids' rotten behavior and whining about how tough it is bringing up kids these days.

The walls are paper-thin in this place, which can be both good and bad, depending on whoever's trying to hide something from the other that day. I overheard that Calvin was only kicked off the bus for four days. It figures; I'm the one getting slammed all the time, while everyone else gets off like they have halos lighting up in neon colors over their angelic little heads.

"Calvin Forbes's mom called me." Her voice doesn't register with me until she starts ladling some of the stew onto my plate. Steam wafts its way up my nose with the mouth-watering smell of basil and onions. That together with the buttered garlic bread I'm now taking out of the oven is making my mouth drool. She sets both plates on the table while I pour out two glasses of fruit juice and plop ice into them.

We start eating, sitting at opposite ends of the small oval kitchen table. As small as it is, it barely fits in the room. Sometimes I think that may be half our problem: we have no real way of giving each other personal space. I can't turn around without my parent right there asking questions; it gets old. Factor that in with another annoyance, namely that I have to pretend not to hear her phone calls, and that's a huge source of irritation.

"Don't you want to know how the conversation went?" Her eyes probe my face for a response.

"Ah, sure," I say. "What did she want?"

"Well, she apologized for Calvin hitting you, and mentioned the swollen jaw and bloody nose he came home with. When she asked if he had been fighting, he said he got knocked into a locker door in the crowded hallway. Then the school called and she found out it was you. So he admitted the fight and told her you got what you deserved."

"She probably apologized because she's afraid you might sue her, but he never landed a single punch," I mumble with my mouth full.

"What did you say?" Her voice is rising. She peers around a grouping of ceramic Halloween pumpkins that are still on the table from doing double duty as Thanksgiving decorations. We had passed a quiet but tense Thanksgiving Day, not happy with each other. The countdown for Christmas has started, but who knows how that will play out, since I seem to attract trouble wherever I go.

"I said he started it, and I don't see why he's only kicked off for four days, while I'm thrown off for the rest of the year." I don't feel like pretending anymore, which causes her a huge sigh of exasperation.

"Were you listening to my phone call, Amber? Anyhow, maybe it has to do with the two fights you were in last month with Casey and Kelly. Unless you are aspiring to be a professional boxer, I suggest this is not what you want for yourself out of life. Lots of kids have it a lot harder than you do, and they manage to stay levelheaded and out of trouble."

Now it's my turn to sigh. "Maybe if they didn't make it their job to spread rumors about me every day, I wouldn't have these problems. You know how much I hate liars." Her face turns fiery red at that, so I hurry and change the subject. "You don't know what school's like these days; things were different back in the day."

"Not that different, really, from what's going on now," she counters. "There have always been the 'cool' kids and 'not so cool' kids." She shoots me a look that ticks me off again. It's bad enough some kids think I'm not cool just because I raise my hand in class occasionally to answer a favorite teacher's questions or wear the same jeans twice in one week. Does my own mother think I'm not cool now too?

"Just look for the kids that have similar interests as you do. Hang out with them and forget about the rest of them."

I grit my teeth and figure she really means well. Mothers just can't grasp how the system works. Rumors take off with lightning speed, what with various "mean girl" websites popping up all over.

Two months ago, two girls hacked into another girl's Instagram page and uploaded nasty pictures to it, complete with her phone number on it. The next thing she knew, she had perverts calling her twenty-four seven. Sadly, the three originally had been friends, so they knew her password. And it all happened just because they'd mistakenly thought she'd stolen one of their boyfriends. Chloe's the only one who has my password, 'cause she's totally trustworthy. But it does save you time when you're not friends with the same kid anymore, to have never given it out in the first place.

And then, as if we don't have enough to worry about from "frenemies," the guys are no better. Just get one mad at you, like an old boyfriend, for example. They're just as likely to put up info on their websites, complete with names and cell phone numbers, of all their ex- girlfriends. How low can you get?

Back in her day, graffiti on bathroom walls or gym lockers was about as bad as it got. How am I supposed to point that out to her without making her feel even more ancient than she is! She comes home complaining about migraines and carpal tunnel syndrome and then expects me to be her best friend. I've had enough for one day. I grab my plate and head for the sink to rinse it.

"Not so fast," she stops me. "We need to go over arrangements to make for you after school, while I'm still at work."

"Chloe's house is five blocks from school. I can stay there when she's not staying after for choir practice."

"Great, but when she has practice, you will have to walk the seven blocks to the library." I'm protesting that it's past Thanksgiving and freezing, but she cuts me off. "These are the consequences of your actions, Amber. You will have to live with them. Don't look at me like that. I've been very open with you about how I had to live with past consequences myself. What with marrying your father so young, without first getting a college education—it was incredibly hard on me when he left us. He was sending money, but it just stopped."

I wish now that I had focused on her puzzlement over the sudden lack of support and communication from Dad. Sadly, all I feel is the sting of her labeling me as her problem. "Yeah, I guess I am just another one of your consequences, huh, Mom?" Her words echo in my head. Did I ask for any of this? "I have a test to study for, since you took my life away from me for the weekend." I spin around and leave her sitting there, her mouth opening and closing like a guppy.

"Amber," she calls after me in a strangled tone as I'm almost to the top of the stairs. "That's not what I meant at all and you know it."

Chapter Eight

YANKING OPEN THE door to my room, I slam it for good measure and then head toward my computer desk, which doubles as a drawing table. I kick the trash basket over, but force myself to unclench my hands, which have somehow curled up into fists. Might as well get started sketching my dad. I have no intention of studying until the last minute, which is normal for me. In the dark, I concentrate hard on calming down before switching on the desk lamp. I remember to download the picture onto a spare memory stick for backup. Squinting to get a better look at them, I find the copies are even blurrier than the originals, but I'll have to make do.

Studying them, I can see he's got strong features: a head of thick dark brown wavy hair, chiseled nose, high forehead, full smile and laughing eyes. He even has what looks like a cleft in his chin, like comic book superheroes do. He's tall and is looking straight into the camera with confidence. Suddenly, it hits me; I look far more like him, minus the height, than I do my mom. I even have a little cleft in my chin too. Our noses are alike as well, but his eyes are darker. Mine are a warm amber color, which accounts for my name.

It's too bad I'm short like my mom, since my dad's height is around six foot two. I could have used a few more inches; people take you more seriously then. It seems pretty random as to how this DNA stuff plays out.

Dad's family background is British, with the name Thomas Wilcox going way back to early times, while my mother's Italian maiden name is Mancini. Her first name is Angelica. All I can say is somewhere between the two of them they managed to produce one hot-tempered kid.

Did I mention she's convinced I have this "warrior gene" thing where you can't help yourself from getting really mad at people? She wanted to get me tested, using a simple swab inside the cheek with a Q-tip and send it in to some lab for the results. Too bad it costs like a thousand dollars!

I start sketching him freehand, working carefully to match the photo. I wish I had a lock on my door and hope she won't barge in without warning. She mostly leaves me alone when I tell her to, but I have my science textbook, which is large enough to cover the picture, just in case.

The only memory I have of my dad is more of a feeling of happier times. I have seen one picture of me riding high on his shoulders, screeching with laughter, my arms opened wide as he twirls me around. That was years back, before she decided to box up all the family pictures that had him in them and hide them away.

I'm starting to imagine things I would ask if I ever find him. Things like: How does a father walk away from his own family, and not even want to watch his kid grow up? Did you ever think I might want a dad around sometimes? You could have at least paid child support, right?

I realize I'm grinding my teeth, another bad habit of mine, and tears are blurring my sight before dropping down onto my drawing like fat raindrops that had been busy building up, creating blotches. Maybe I shouldn't bother trying to find out the truth.

But any number of things might have happened, I tell myself. Things like: what if he got sick and couldn't keep in touch with Mom? Or maybe he hit his head and has amnesia; I know that one's a long shot. Maybe he even has an addiction and is living on the streets of downtown Columbus.

Things happen all the time to people that they never figured would happen. That homeless guy who sounded like a D.J. got to reunite with his family. They all ended up on the *Dr. Phil Show*, my mom's favorite show. Everyone deserves that, even my dad, right?

In Dad's case, Mom might not agree, even though her favorite saying is "Don't judge a book by its cover." She figures I should relate to that since I love reading and I love illustrating my term papers by hand. When she mentioned that saying in the same breath she used to refer to Kelly and Casey, I flipped.

She's been harping lately that I should have a heart-to-heart with them outside of school, because the school professionals told her bringing us into the same room would be counterproductive. They're the bullies, but somehow their parents think I am. How twisted is that? If I could "hold a meeting" with them after school, it would be somewhere in some back alley! Then I could let them know what I really think about their back-stabbing ways!

Imagine if I wrote in to her favorite doctor dude show, mentioning my long-lost dad and how Mom should have a heart-to-heart with him, if he ever shows up, about why he walked out on her? How would she feel then? I bet she'd rearrange his "book cover" for him. There'd be fireworks going off for sure!

Out of the corner of my eye I see a message flashing, and Chloe's chat box pops up again.

Chloe: what's up?

(We always use lower case to type faster.)

Me: drawing and daydreaming. have to start over on my picture but will have it done by the end of tomorrow. how did your rehearsal go for winter fest?

Chloe: practicing more to nail it down, but it will turn out okay. do you think your mom will let me come over sunday afternoon after our family's brunch?

Me: not sure if I can talk her into it. she's really mad at me. school wants another conference. might be kicked out for good.

Chloe: not probable.

Me: hope you're right. calvin only got four days.

Chloe: he's a jerk. tell your mom we have to study.

Me: i'll try. how fast can we get a website up?

Chloe: we should just use facebook. faster that way. i'll help you put up the stats and check out replies by checking their own page out first. we won't post any personal pics. will work out how they can leave you a message. if we used a real url, you would have to pay like $13.00 a month on a credit card account, so fb is better.

Me: makes sense. i don't have money to burn. mom won't get me a credit card. she says credit card companies are like slaveholders and use us as their slaves.

Chloe: weird! but, whatever. let me know how it goes. we are getting ready to go to a movie. bye for now.

Me: k. later.

There's a knock on my door and I quickly cover the now-stained drawing with the book and minimize my screen. Mom is trying to be respectful, so I grudgingly tell her to come in.

"I have to grocery shop. Do you want to come?" I am in no mood for her peace offering, but maybe I can wheedle my way into having Chloe over if I do.

"I guess so. I need shampoo and other stuff you usually forget to get me."

"You can make a list up while I cut out some coupons. That together with my store card will save us some money. We'll shop for the month, which will let me save twenty cents a gallon at the gas pumps." She's thinking out loud about money as usual and is already headed downstairs. I sigh and trail after the

Coupon Queen, wishing we didn't have to account for every single cent every minute of our lives.

It's a wonder she could afford to buy us a laptop and me a phone. I suppose brown-bagging school lunch and going to dollar movies or the RedBox helped. Yard sales loom large in our lives in the summer. Now, since winter is almost here, she's got me going to discount stores, or waiting until things go on sale. Not such great fun shopping for end of the season summer stuff, knowing it's getting too cold to wear any of it.

We get stuck out in the additional parking area at Giant Eagle and even there she gets beat out of a couple of spots, which makes her mumble something unmentionable under her breath. Just goes to show you how many other people don't have lives on a Friday night besides us. We have to run to keep ourselves from turning into ice popsicles in the gusty wind. And of course snow has to be coming down in huge chunks. I grab a runaway cart right before it rolls straight into the side of an SUV.

A random thought about how terrible it would be to have to live on the streets on a night like this pops into my head. The weather forecast is for blizzard conditions all night. In my heart of hearts, I hope my dad isn't out there, homeless and on the streets.

Once inside, we make quick work of going up and down the aisles, with me trying to pick the right moment to ask about Chloe coming over. Timing is everything when it comes to getting what you want from parents, especially if you're in my situation. We're standing in the all-important candy aisle, because she's stopped drinking wine now. This is probably due to how I embarrassed her by telling Dr. Bug Eyes that she drinks too much.

She's deciding between dark chocolate with 80% cocoa, which is hugely caffeinated but low in sugar, or a bag of Hershey's Kisses. She picks the dark, insisting it has more healthy antioxidants. I select my usual Kit Kats and toss them into the cart. It's now or never before she starts comparing unit prices or reading food labels.

"Mom, I've got to get Chloe's help in studying for the science test. She says she can come over after her family's Sunday brunch."

Chloe's mom makes the best egg and sausage casserole ever, with yummy blueberry muffins and hot cocoa with real whipped cream on the side. My mouth waters just remembering the last time they had me over.

What a scrumptious spread for her family. Chloe, her parents, and her little brother are usually all home for meals. Her parents are actually fun; they laugh and joke around. It's obvious they really love each other too and would never think of splitting up. Chloe is so lucky with her year-round tan, her salon nails, plus her perfect family. Heck, even her eleven-year-old brother is a great athlete and acts really cool to her. Their house is gorgeous and looks like it should be on some HGTV show. In contrast, I have no siblings, Mom doesn't even like to cook, and our apartment is decorated in what she terms the "shabby chic" style. It's a good thing I'm not the jealous type!

Mom frowns. "No way, Amber. Not after everything that has happened today."

"You could at least give me some credit for trying to turn my grades around. Any other parent would be doing back flips by now. I really need her help." I can tell she's wavering. I try looking as cute and helpless as possible, like that Puss in Boots cat in the movie *Shrek*. You'd have to really hate cats to resist the face on that kitty.

"I will make you a deal," she says, eyeing me steadily. "You'll have to promise to follow Dr. Jenkins's instructions to the letter tomorrow. Whatever he suggests, you have to promise to try. You can count on me doing my part. I need to know you will do yours. I'm really on your side, honey."

"Sure, fine."

Evidently, she doesn't hear enough enthusiasm to suit her. "I mean it, Amber. Like it or not, we are in this together. Do we have a deal?"

"I get it, for real. I don't like exploding all the time, trust me."

"Okay, then let's call a truce. From now on, we work together." Mom has thrown in several more bags of goodies between our little talk, enough to last a year. I like this new mom who's switched out her nightly glass of wine for candy she can share with me. Obviously, chocolate must be her new method for stress reduction. Too bad it doesn't do that for me. And I refuse to think about the cavities it could be causing us down the road. While I push our dental health out of my mind, she heads for the checkout, talking nonstop.

"Believe it or not, it's not always easy for me to keep my temper either." Oh, I can believe that all right! Better not go there though. And I can't help wondering how long this "togetherness" will last, either.

On the way out, we stop at the Red Box in the store's lobby. It takes a long time to agree on something, but we settle on an old classic, *Water for Elephants*, with Robert Pattinson. He's sporting a healthy tan in this movie, unlike his vampire days in his movie *Twilight*.

Thinking of tanning, if she would give me an allowance for doing chores, I could afford to go tanning like half the girls in my classes. Of course she has to think it's unhealthy because of some scientific research and says I would be a shriveled-up prune with skin cancer by the time I'm thirty. She's so overprotective. Besides that, I should help out around the house for nothing, because she can't keep up with it all and "every family member should have chores." What happened to the idea of kids having fun in their teen years, without a care in the world?

After I help carry in and put the groceries away, she makes popcorn. We settle in next to each other on the couch. It's like the old days before I read her diary. I wish I'd never looked inside it. Almost, that is. But "the truth will out," which is a famous quote by Shakespeare, from *The Merchant of Venice*, according to my English teacher. She reads us a quote from a famous author every day to have us use our "critical thinking skills," as she terms it, for "meaningful comprehension."

What I'm starting to comprehend is that nothing ever stays the same and "nothing is but thinking makes it so," quoting her friend Shakespeare again. I let myself think of a better future, a day that might include a father from long ago. I put my head down on Mom's shoulder, letting go without worrying about anything, floating off to sleep before the movie ends.

Chapter Nine

SUNLIGHT ATTACKS MY face, making me throw my arm over my eyes. But now I'm being bombarded by the sounds of opening and shutting drawers and sizzling bacon and eggs, smells which tantalize me. I give up trying to will myself back to sleep and sit up, bleary-eyed, rubbing at my neck because I slept on it the wrong way. I shuffle into the kitchen to see Mom pouring orange juice. She sees me and hands me a glass, which I take without thanking her.

"You're welcome," she says for me.

"I can't believe you let me sleep on the couch all night," I grumble as I gulp it down and then help put out plates and forks. "My neck hurts. Why didn't you wake me up and tell me to go to bed?"

"Did you just hear yourself?" She's laughing. "What would be the point of that? You were already out like Sleeping Beauty. It made better sense to just put Grandma's quilt around you and pile a couple more blankets on top.

"Are you hungry?" She doesn't give me a chance to answer before adding, "By the way, I have to go into work for a few hours today to make up for all the lost time. I'll be back in time for our appointment with Dr. Jenkins." She throws me a meaningful look on both counts.

I scrunch up my face at that. "Oh joy."

"Amber, remember our deal," she warns. "And while you are waiting for me, maybe you can throw in a load of wash. Also, can you please tidy up the kitchen?" she asks, looking at her watch. "I really need to get going here."

"Great, I will play Cinderella until you get back from the ball." I help myself to some more bacon and slouch back to the table. She stops on her way out to massage my neck, getting the kinks out for me.

"I never heard of a Cinderella who has her own 'wicked' stepmom, or in this case her very own mother, cooking breakfast and rubbing her sore neck before she goes off to this ball called work, especially on a Saturday."

"Ha-ha." I smile my thanks.

It takes some time before I hear the car crunching its way slowly down the icy street. Nobody bothers to plow around here. She had to scrape heavy ice off the car and dig herself out first, when the snowstorm hit hard, since there aren't any garages in this crummy apartment complex. What makes it all worse is that the weather is hardly ever this severe this early. It's not even Christmas yet. As I finish eating, I have been plotting what I need to accomplish before she returns.

After a shower and throwing the laundry in, I start tearing the place up systematically for any clues or paperwork she might still have on my dad. I need exact dates like his birthday, their marriage license, something... I feel like a spy, or worse yet, a thief, but I have already tried to ask for more details about him. She says she's talked enough about him for now, and just changes the subject.

Going through her overloaded closet is like going on an archeological dig; it takes almost an hour. I have to be careful to put everything back the way it was. I come up empty-handed and discouraged. It looks like she deleted every trace of him. I flop down on the floor next to her bed, picking idly at some dust bunnies I kicked up when it occurs to me to look under the bed. A story about how Grandma stuck tons of recipes torn out of old magazines under her bed comes to mind. Maybe Mom has carried on the tradition, but it wouldn't be recipes, because she has a bunch of cookbooks taking up half the already small counter space, leaving hardly any room to actually prepare anything. I stretch my arm as far underneath as I can, hoping there are no spiders around, even hoping they go dormant during the winter. There's no real guarantee about that and I have a phobia about creepy crawlies. My hand falls on paperwork of some kind. I haul it out in the open. Eureka! It is a bunch of old letters tied up with a fancy ribbon. Undoing them, I see some are from Dad, others are replies from Mom.

They are dated from the early 2000s. I was born in 2006 and Mom and Dad were both born in 1987, which means they were crazy young when Mom was expecting me.

Now I really feel like a spy. Trying not to read them, I look at the dates. They go back to the early nineties. Mom did make a point of saying she was only nineteen when they got married, so he couldn't have been that much older, right?

Greedy for any scraps of my dad's life, I break down and start skimming through the letters. By the fifth one, I have a definite lump in my throat. They are remembering back to when they were childhood sweethearts, having known each other from the sixth grade on. There is a dried out red rose tucked inside one letter where he talks about their senior prom as the day he fell in love with her.

In another letter she talks about his birthday on May ninth, laughing about how he's dating an older woman because she's two weeks older than he is. I know she's thirty-three, so she must have been expecting me when they got married. This was one more reason for Grandpa's chronic crabbiness: he had to pay for a wedding, Mom was expecting and nobody had a job!

Proving, I guess, that the lyric from the old Beatles song she loves so much, "Love is all you need," is not necessarily accurate, even though as a teenager my mother believed otherwise in one of her letters to Dad. Plus she sometimes still hums it. Wow! Reality bites!

My mouth drops open when I read the last letter.

My Dearest Angel,

Because of what we just found out, I think strongly we should keep this to ourselves until after the wedding. By then the dust will have settled and your parents will be better equipped to handle the idea of becoming grandparents. I am overjoyed and scared all at the same time with what we have been entrusted with. I have my doubts about being a decent dad to our unborn child, but with your help, I'll do my best. June 20th cannot come fast enough for me. You are my world, my angel, you and now our child on the way. What an adventure it will be.

Your scared witless husband-to-be,

Thomas

Truthfully, I had always suspected this was the case, but confirming it makes me feel like I'm skydiving, with my insides dropping like a stone. I try and imagine what Mom must have felt like when she first found out. How hard to try and keep something like this from one's own parents. I wonder if she had a BFF of her own to confide in.

I'm getting teary-eyed, so before they fall and made telltale splatters on the letters, I bind them back up and put them away where I found them. My eyes scan the room, making sure everything is just the way it was when I first went in. I even pick up the dust bunnies disturbed while rummaging through the closet. Satisfied I've done my best to cover my tracks, I quietly close her door and go into my own room.

I shut the door, not knowing how much longer I have before she comes home. I really need to shift the wet clothes over to the dryer, but I also have to get the picture of my dad done. Somehow, it seems to come together much faster than before. I'm putting on the final touches when I hear tires crunching along the unsalted street. Not too many other cars are moving the morning after a blizzard, so I think it's her. Twitching the curtain aside to look out since my bedroom window faces the street, I see I'm right.

Dashing downstairs, I switch the clothes over, turning on the dryer just as she comes through the door. Mom looks like she'd really like to kick back a while, but we have to be sure we have enough time to make it across town. The highway is terrible right after a storm, so her driving will be cautious to the point of crawling along.

"Amber, let's go," she says in a tired tone, not bothering to even shut the front door. Gusts of icy wind invade the living room and set the windows to rattling.

"Okay." I slam the door to the tiny laundry closet and grab a jacket from the hall closet diagonally across from the rattling old dryer.

"And can you scoop up a couple of apples from the fruit bowl, so we have something to snack on while I drive?"

I dart into the kitchen after them and add a couple of nutrition bars as well.

She locks the door and we're off, snacking silently for the most part, until some nut who thinks 270 North is a NASCAR track regardless of bad weather swerves into our lane, nearly cutting us off. Mom goes off on the guy, slamming her hand hard on the horn. That's some pretty impressive road rage she's got there. I wonder who needs counseling more, between the two of us. We arrive ten minutes late, but thankfully still all in one piece.

Chapter Ten

AHHHHH. NOTHING LIKE breathing in the aroma of dirty old sneakers as Dr. Bug Eyes tells me to sit back and relax. He talks in an informational monotone.

"The thing to watch for is how you react when you first start getting upset, Amber. Are you clenching your hands, and tensing your muscles? Is your stomach feeling tied up in knots right before you lose your temper? These are the signs to look for. They are reactions to whatever is triggering your anxiety." He continues to drone on.

"Triggers are patterns of thoughts or situations you know happen over and over. For example, the two girls in your class who tick you off. That is a situation trigger. Do you tend to think negative thoughts about them, or think of them as always wrong and yourself as always right? Those thoughts are triggers as well. Nobody is ever all wrong or right. Your rational mind should know this has to be the case."

Hmm. What else should my rational brain know?

"So, Amber, when that happens, you need to realize the thought pattern you are in is what we call the 'all or nothing pattern,' and learn not go to extremes, but to think more rationally."

He continues, "I want you to try an exercise. First, tighten up your jaw, fists and shoulders. Now relax them. Can you feel the difference? Even if you can keep your face relaxed when you start getting upset, it will be harder to stay angry as long as usual. My suggestion is to force your face to relax and not glare at people. Then breathe slowly and deeply from your diaphragm, like a singer, to completely fill your lungs. Count out loud if you have to in between breaths."

I am sure that would be a source of great amusement to the girl bullies. But he's still talking. "What good is it if your body is relaxing, but your mind isn't calming down? You need to instruct it by telling yourself 'I can relax' or 'I will stay in control.' This is going to take practice. Do you have any questions at this point?"

"Well, yeah. I can't stand knowing they're breathing the same air as me, and wish they'd drop dead. How do I stop that?"

Old Doc Jenkins gives me his usual smirk. "You don't have to like them, just be respectful. I have a little list for you of do's and don'ts." He shuffles through his papers. He wasn't kidding. "Let's look this over together," he says. I force myself to look down at the paper he shoves under my nose.

DOS

- Show respect to others.
- Listen carefully to what others say.
- Look for things to appreciate in others.
- Speak in a quiet voice.
- Stop criticizing, name-calling and insulting others.

DON'TS

- Don't make fun of anyone.
- Don't roll your eyes or make faces.
- Don't call people names.

Unbelievable! My eyes are glazing over, but I lie and say I will review it again later. His mouth lifts in a genuine smile, the first I've seen in a month of our "getting-to-know-you sessions," as he calls them.

"I can guarantee if you try a few of these tips at a time, you won't be feeling like you are about to burst, Amber. Keep a log or journal. Label it 'My Feelings' and note down how you feel each day and what you did to help yourself feel better.

"By the way, I will ask your mother to do the same thing." My ears perk up at this. "This isn't about 'fixing' only you, or your mother either, but about giving you both strategies to use in rough times." He leans back in his cushy chair, watching me jiggle my foot. "What do you think? Does it make sense?"

"It's a lot to remember," I say truthfully. "What if it doesn't work? Besides, they might kick me out of school anyway." I just have to get him off my back somehow.

"Not if I let them know we are working on the issues. Your mother informed me about the meeting on Monday. The school team will see you are setting your goals in the following areas: getting your grades back up, managing your impulse control and your anxiety levels."

"Yeah, okay. I'll give it try. It might be just part of my DNA, you know. My mom heard about this 'warrior gene' stuff on TV and thought it described me for sure."

He breaks out in a loud guffaw. "It's more likely it's an ingrained habit, rather than a part of your structural makeup. A lot more research has to be done before it can be determined if the so-called 'warrior gene' is the definitive factor related to anger issues. Instead of worrying about uncontrollable genes, just work on using the strategies we talked about to calm your body down. Things will get better; you'll see.

"Think it over while I talk with your mom. You'll both be working together on this." He makes sure I have my list plus a worksheet summary of strategies, and he makes sure Mom gets her own copy. Armed with that, we are to go forth and conquer.

If only life were that easy.

Chapter Eleven

ARRIVING HOME FROM our appointment, Mom announces she's exhausted and even turns off her phone to take a nap. I tell her I will make dinner soon; taco salads will be easy to fix. This should give me plenty of time to write up a list of all the information I now have about my father. I know his date of birth, plus the date of marriage, because he wrote about it in the last letter I read. They talked about keeping their secret, meaning me, from everyone: the grandparents and both sets of parents, until he could get a steady job.

It was a June wedding at the Park of Roses in Clintonville. She referred back to it from time to time in her diary, lamenting how something so right could turn out so wrong. Too bad she hadn't just told me the actual date, which would have spared me going into the spy business.

According to her diary, rain had threatened their outdoor wedding, but the clouds had parted as they spoke their vows. A shaft of sunlight had lit up the rose-covered arbor they stood in as if lighting up a stage. She commented on how Dad had said she was indeed his sweet angel, and always would be.

I press my pencil so hard on the pad that it breaks. I'd been imagining the fragrant roses. In a way I had been at their wedding, nestled in between them as they pledged their forever love to each other. Maybe Mom was right, and many men really couldn't be counted on, starting with boys. I thought Calvin and I were really going to be going together at one point, before his buddies convinced him I was nuts.

I finish my list of statistics I'll need for setting up a site, including questions I have for Chloe when I see her tomorrow. Glancing at the clock, I see it's time to start dinner. I hide my list under the same trusty big book and go downstairs.

Now it's my turn to start banging cupboards and pots around as I cook up the ground beef and chop onions and green peppers. I cut up tomatoes, shred cheese and rinse the lettuce. The pre-formed taco shells are quickly turning too brown, so I yank them out fast, knocking my wrist on the hot rack. I let loose with a loud, "Crap." Focused as I am on the pain, I don't notice her standing in the doorway, her hair all messed up from her "power nap on the couch." Her only comment is, "Run cold water over it, quick." She makes her way to the fridge and pulls out the salsa, asking me if I want root beer or orange, while popping the salsa into the microwave to warm it.

After soaking my wrist, I see the narrow burn slash isn't so bad, so I pull up a chair and start adding the salsa, which melts the cheese under it perfectly. I shove in a huge bite and manage to burn my tongue. Just then I remember I need to know my mom's plans for tomorrow, so Chloe and I can work on the website in peace.

"What have you got going on when Chloe comes over tomorrow?" I ask pointedly, after slurping my drink to soothe my throbbing tongue. She stops chewing in surprise, and then smiles knowingly.

"Oh, you mean I am supposed to be elsewhere? I might bring back that bunch of overdue books to the library, now that it's stopped snowing. The roads should be better by then or at least not as bad as today. I won't be gone the whole afternoon, though, so you'll have to put up with me, like it or not. Remember, you weren't supposed to be having anyone over, Amber."

"I was just asking, jeez!" I try to look hurt. "We'll be holed up in my room anyway, studying for the science test and stuff."

"Right," she says with a little frown pulling down the corners of her mouth. "It's the 'stuff' part that I'm worried about. I was a teenager once myself, you know."

"Why do you always have to act so suspicious of everything I do?"

"Please don't start something that you are in no position to finish." She's puffing her cheeks out which are turning a rosy color. "I'm just thinking you seem to be protesting a bit too much, if all you both want to do is study."

"Mom, hold on. We are not supposed to be getting on each other's nerves, remember?"

"And maybe you should remember that I am cutting you some slack when I shouldn't be. So make sure you aren't on the internet for any other reason except to look up information of the studying kind."

"You worry too much."

"Hmm," she says, backing off, before getting up to rummage through the pantry looking for her stash of chocolate to help calm her nerves.

Great. Her "Mom radar" is on high alert, so how am I supposed to get around her restrictions about the computer? Well, I will have to think of something. I deposit my plate and glass into the sink and head into the living room just to get away, leaving her to clean up the mess.

I rummage through the DVDs for something to watch. She cut out the cable a month ago, temporarily she said, to help make the bill paying more manageable. She says Netflix might be next, because it costs nine dollars a month. Terrific! Between that and not being old enough to drive, I'm feeling completely claustrophobic. If I had a car, I'd be miles away by now.

I finally settle on *Confessions of a Shopaholic*. Mom said it was another "oldie but goodie," and she picked it out a while back supposedly to prove the pitfalls of overusing one's credit cards. Since she can't afford to let me have one, and wouldn't if she could, I don't see the point of the "teachable" moment she was hoping for. Still, it's good for some laughs and I sure can use some. She joins me after a while and we sit together, idly picking away at some leftover cookies while giggling at the goofy choices the "Girl with the Green Scarf" keeps making.

My mind's too keyed up to fall asleep before it ends this time. I start making a mental list of everything I need to get the web page up and running.

Tomorrow I'm placing my plan into action, and like a stone creating concentric circles in a pond, I can only hope the ripple effect will cause many unforeseen repercussions.

Chapter Twelve

I WAKE UP early, to a cold house and weak sunlight, which is inadequate to begin melting the stubborn ice-covered streets and roads. No lounging around for me. I have to be ready for when Chloe comes over later. I throw open some textbooks and find my notebook that has the study guide for the test. I go downstairs to stick a Pop-Tart into the toaster and grab juice, all while whispering to Chloe on my newly returned phone. Lucky for me, she is always an early riser. She confirms we are still a go after her family has brunch, and I exhale a huge sigh of relief. I turn around and see a scary sight: Mom standing in the doorway with a bad case of bed head, squinting in the sunlight streaming in from the little window over the sink.

"Amber, what are you doing up so early? Your banging around down here woke me up!" She's clearly ticked, since neither of us gets up before ten on a typical Sunday. Blast this rat hole; I really thought I was being quiet.

To take her mind off things I ask if she wants me to make her something. Wrong move. Now she's really suspicious.

"What are you up to exactly? You've never offered to make breakfast for me in your life!"

I laugh like she said something hilarious. "Well, there's always a first time for everything."

"Hmm, I'll play along for now. No sense turning down a free breakfast!" She plops down and asks for eggs over easy while watching, amused, as I scramble around, trying to find the spatula and crack eggs on the edge of the frying pan at the same time.

Then I forget to spray the pan and have to dig them out when they're done. Mom wisely keeps a straight face when I place her plate in front of her. I remind her about Chloe coming over.

"Gotcha. I'm meeting a friend for early lunch; then I'll be at the library, plus maybe do a little Christmas shopping." I smile at that because it means she'll hit all the dollar stores she can find, looking for cheap stocking stuffers. Hey, if it keeps her occupied long enough for us to get the website up, I'm good with that. We retreat to our bedrooms after breakfast, like two boxers going into separate corners.

Once she leaves the house, I can upload the picture from the file again onto my phone and from there to the new website. I can hear her banging her drawers and then her closet door, trying to find something clean to wear. She's just as bad as I am at remembering to throw in a wash or move it to the dryer. Finally, she knocks on my door and tells me she's going.

"I'll have my cell on, if you need anything. Also, there's frozen pizza that you can make for lunch; just don't burn the house down doing it."

I force a smile and wave her off. Why does she say stupid stuff like that every chance she gets?

"Yeah, thanks. We'll be fine. See you later."

I get another one of those probing mom looks and then she's gone. I don't move until I hear her car going down the street. I keep sitting there in case she's forgotten something and has to come back. Believe me, it's happened before.

Now I'm up and feeling tense, but excited. I mentally go over everything I need in order to make the plan come together in the time we'll have to work with.

While waiting for Chloe, I decide to put a backup of the picture and what the website info will say onto a memory stick. There it will stay, in case I have to delete the picture of my drawing on my phone. Next, I nervously check the bio I wrote about my dad. Nothing too specific, since anyone responding will be required to fill in a lot of details and prove he is who he says he is. I puzzle over which email address to use for a possible contact and decide to open a new Yahoo one. Mom had made me give over my password to my Hotmail, so this will hopefully throw her off the track, if need be. I run my fingers through my hair and then realize I forgot to take a shower. By the time I'm done, Chloe will be here. I give a last look around, then grab my makeup stuff and hurry off to get ready.

Chapter Thirteen

SHOWERED, BLOW-DRIED, and changed, I'm shaking out my hair and pulling it into a quick ponytail when I hear the doorbell ring. I rush downstairs to yank the door open. A blast of polar air invites itself in as Chloe holds the door open while waving goodbye to her mom.

She turns and shoves a casserole dish into my hands. "Leftovers for later; now let's get started!"

I take one look at the enticing sausage and egg casserole, complete with a side of banana bread, and head straight for the microwave with Chloe snickering at me the whole time. I have a plate ready and waiting when the timer goes off. I start to get a plate for her too, but she waves me off, grumbling that we don't have all day. Shrugging, I take my plate and fork and tuck the whole casserole under one arm, lagging behind long enough to shove one hot bite in my mouth. She takes the stairs two at a time, walking straight into my room and over to the computer. Chloe reads the bio about my dad out loud:

Wanted: Information about my missing dad

I'm looking for my dad, Thomas Wilcox, born May 9th, 1987. He went missing in 2010, when I was just four. His last known address was in the Short North or Brewery District of Columbus, Ohio. Anyone with knowledge of him or with a picture of him that looks like the photo above should contact me at the following email address: awilcox37@yahoo.com

If you claim to actually be him, you must include my mom's maiden name and the nickname you had for her. You must also list your occupation at the time you left us. If you just think you recognize the man in this drawing or know of his whereabouts, give him this email address and let him know I am trying to find him.

Sincerely,
A. Wilcox- daughter of a deadbeat dad

Chloe makes a noise after reading what I wrote. I can't tell if she's snorting or laughing deep in her throat.

"What?" I ask, puzzled.

"I think you can leave that last part out, about being the daughter of a deadbeat dad, I mean. Everything else should work. If you drive home the point of him being a deadbeat, you run the risk of him or his friends not replying to the missing person page. Now first, we'll get on your web page and hit the create page button. Then we will follow the prompts and click on the icon." She works rapidly as she tells me what she's doing. "That will be our Facebook connection page. Later we will create a missing person listing on NamUs. This organization can spread your dad's picture all over the U.S. However, let's do first things first with the Facebook page. Okay, so far so good," she reassures herself. "Let's just follow the prompts." We do. "Next, upload your picture of your dad, Amber." We do this first for the new Facebook page and scrutinize it as it pops up. It comes out clean, with dark lines and good shading.

"Great! Now go ahead and type your bio post, minus the daughter of a deadbeat, that is," she says, smirking. "You also have to type in the country besides the city and state, plus the month and day he went missing. Just put what you do know for sure instead of guessing at it." I blink hard, trying to remember everything she says.

"I'm worried about your contact email. Maybe include the police station's contact page, because otherwise you might get pranked, Amber. Or some weirdo hacker might get your personal page or even find out where you and your mom live. Maybe if you ask that the police contact us, weirdos won't be so fast to leave troll comments."

I rapidly suck air into my lungs, which feel like they're being starved for oxygen, freaking out over the possibility some stalker might find us. Chloe looks at me, concerned. "Amber, don't you dare hyperventilate, not now," she orders. "Breathe slowly in and out through your nose."

Becoming annoyed at her commands, I start to even out my breathing so I can talk. "Stop sounding like Dr. Jenkins, for crying out loud!"

Chloe isn't listening. She's busy finding the email address for the Columbus Police, which she has me add, along with the Yahoo address. "Good," she declares, breathing out a sigh of relief after I change it.

"Another free thing we can do is to go onto a Missing Person Alert Page, which is already set up on Facebook, and place info about your dad there too."

I stare at her in amazement. "How do you know all this stuff?" She grins and reminds me of her friend in the choir whose dog had been lost for over a month. "This is a little more complicated than that, but the same basic idea! And she told me she wanted to post everywhere she possibly could think of. She found her sweet puppy being creative like you are doing!" Chloe turns back to the laptop screen. "Do you want to make any more changes before you hit the 'Create Page'?"

I'm staring so hard at everything, going over and over it in my mind. My mouth is so dry I can hardly get the words out. I swallow hard and then whisper, "Do it."

Instead, she gets up and makes me sit in the hot seat. "You do the honors," she insists. "It's your idea and your page." We look at each other, not daring to speak.

It feels like time has stopped for a few nervous seconds. My hand is shaking. Then in one quick stroke of the mouse, I hit the "create" icon. It's done. All my desperate hopes and a part of my life history are now spinning out into cyberspace for who knows how long or how many clicks from unknown people who happen to see it. Maybe it will shine like a lighthouse beacon that my dad will find somehow. I feel as if, through sheer willpower, I am forcing a connection to exist between my lost father and me.

Chapter Fourteen

CHLOE AND I both exhale at the same time. Turns out she's been holding her breath too. We both stare at the page, especially at his picture.

"He really does look like he could just start walking and talking. I don't know how you do it, Amber. You should really go to the Columbus Art School downtown after we finish high school."

I tear my eyes away from my drawing to look at her. The spell is officially broken. "I don't know," I say. "It's so expensive and they only give you a break the first year with the scholarship, hoping you will keep going even if you don't qualify for another, 'cause you have to be that crazy good. Then I'll be stuck paying back student loans for the rest of my life. Plus, I'm not into animation or fashion design. Maybe I could learn to do digital art, even though you know how dumb I am with computers."

"That's why you would go to college there, to learn that all that, silly." We both grin. It feels good to lighten up.

"Yeah, well, what about yourself? You have an awesome voice. You should go to music school or try out for *American Idol* or something. Either that or computers; you're amazing at both." I watch as she opens up the Missing Person Alert page on Facebook and types the needed info about my dad there too.

I feel a sudden stab of jealousy. With inborn talents plus money from her folks, Chloe has a clear road ahead of her. Case in point: last month we were both drooling over some cool cars we'd seen displayed at the mall and filling out the sweepstake coupon cards with our parents' names and numbers, just for fun. Chloe said this would help clue her parents in about what kind of car they could get her when she turned sixteen. She was being serious. Thing is, she has no reason not to be; all her dreams stand a good chance of coming true. I would have to win a lottery to make mine happen. I let out huge sigh thinking about how different our lives are.

She tilts her head to one side and presses her mouth together, puzzled. "What are you thinking now?" For as long as I've known her she's had that funny habit.

"Oh, nothing much," I reply. "Maybe we better save the other websites for next time. There are so many possible resources to help find my dad, but I do have to study for that science test. We need to make sure someone's Mom radar doesn't go off when she gets back. Let's get all this cleaned up and out of sight, so she won't have any cause to wonder what we've been doing."

"Yeah, time to remove the evidence." She laughs and starts gathering all the papers into a pile while I look under the casserole dish to find the chapter review questions for us to go over. Then I remember I only had time for one bite of the yummy brunch, since Chloe went right to work on the...special project, as I'm calling it. Even now, I can hardly believe what we have just done. I am torn between trying to concentrate on tectonic plates and continental drift and running down to the microwave to pop in a plate of yummy casserole. My grumbling stomach wins out. I grab my plate and ask Chloe if she wants something to drink or snack on. She gives me a thumbs up, still absorbed in the review questions. Another difference between us: her focus is superb. Mine, not so much—unless it's for art or food.

I race downstairs and toss in my plate into the microwave, which gives me a minute to rummage through the cupboards for snacks. Then I remember she will only want healthy stuff, so I slam the doors shut and start rooting through the refrigerator, looking for what passes for healthy in our house. I find a few semi-wilted celery sticks and some peanut butter. The micro-wave is dinging, so it will have to do. I find sodas and add them to the small tray, which is now overloaded and unbalanced. I wobble my way back upstairs and manage to set it on the desk without sending anything flying to the floor. Chloe looks at the tray and scrunches up her nose.

"Where's the napkins? We can't study with sticky hands." Seeing my dirty look, she flashes her brightest smile. "It's all good; I'll get them," she reassures me. "You just start looking over the questions and see if there's anything I forgot. I circled the ones we really need to go over."

We are still slaving away with the review when Mom comes back, hands full with bags from the dollar store. She sends a cheery hello up to us and asks how everything is going. I heard the car coming, so I am already standing at the head of the stairs as she comes in. Meanwhile, Chloe's giving the room the once over for anything we might have missed while putting away our "special project."

Mom is busy stashing stuff out of sight, but stocking stuffers are easy to spot in a tiny place like ours.

"Would you look at the time?" she says, as if that will distract me from her attempt to cram the bags into the already jammed-full front hall closet. "Is Chloe staying for supper?"

Chloe appears in the doorway of my room, giving me the all-clear, but shaking her head at the invitation. "We're going ice skating tonight, but thanks anyway." She hands me the empty casserole dish and scoops up her book bag, purse and jacket. Her phone is buzzing as we make our way downstairs. I plop the dish down into the sink, run the water and squirt some dish soap in it while Chloe checks her phone and throws her jacket on.

"My mom is on her way over," she says. "I will be so glad when we get our Christmas break next Tuesday. Between all the tests they slam us with and extra choir practices, I am completely fried." She blows a big breath up toward her bangs. "I can't wait to just sleep in for a whole day!"

"Well, another time, then," Mom says, opening up the freezer. "I see you didn't eat the pizza I left for you." She looks over at me puzzled. "I guess that's what we will have for supper." I show her the empty casserole dish from Chloe's mom that I've cleaned and have now been drying right in front of her nose. Her mind is miles away, but she complains when I do the same to her.

Crunching tires and a car honking let Chloe know her mom has arrived. She is determined to shove the casserole dish into her book bag, and finally succeeds by removing our huge science book. I open the door and turn on the outside light. Light snow is starting to come down again, doing a sparkling dance in the light of the doorway.

"Thanks for letting me come over and study with Amber today, Mrs. Wilcox. We got a lot done, didn't we, Amber?" She flashes a knowing smile at me as she goes out. I return it, satisfied that I followed through on my intentions to leave no stone unturned in finding my dad.

"See you tomorrow." I wave as Mom cautions Chloe about the slippery stoop and walkway. "Sorry I didn't find the time to shovel yet."

Chloe yells, "Not a problem," and waves again as she hops into the car. Her mom gives the horn a friendly beep as they head out to pick up the rest of her family.

I plop into a kitchen chair, exhausted, and now thinking about the upcoming school conference, which might end with me being kicked out of school for good. I watch with a furrowed brow as Mom puts the pizza into the oven.

"Are you feeling ready for tomorrow's meeting and your science test?" she asks.

I nod listlessly. Which one should I worry about most: the paper test, or the one being set up by the team of teachers and guidance counselor, including Dr. Jenkins? For that test, I'd better perform like a monkey, so as not to get expelled from school. "I'm worried about everything," I hear myself say.

The upcoming team conference at 8:00 sharp is actually making my stomach churn. What if they decide to kick me out for good? Maybe Dr. Jenkins won't be able to convince them that I can play nice with the mean girls. Not that I really see any reason why I should, since I seem to be the only one who's being made to play nice, as far as I can tell.

Mom is too busy checking on the pizza to notice how quiet I've become.

"Maybe some hot cocoa would be just the ticket on a night like this." She gets some mugs and empties Swiss Miss packs into them. She heats up hot water in the microwave and tells me to add it to the powered cocoa mix in each mug. "And now to get a salad going." She talks to herself as she hustles about the tiny kitchen.

I finish mixing the hot cocoa and get the table set. I try to keep my mind off it all by wondering if there's been any activity on the web page yet. Has someone left a comment about seeing my dad around? Or possibly he himself has somehow seen his name and picture? Will he try and contact me after all these years?

I am flipping out between thinking about school and now about what might or might not be going on with the new web page. Thankfully, she's still oblivious to my mood, so I finish eating and say I'm going upstairs to read and maybe do some drawing. She yawns and tells me she's going to write in her Feelings Journal and suggests I do the same.

"It will take away some of the anxiety, Amber, like Dr. Jenkins said."

"I'll do it later, okay? I just want to relax right now."

"That's fine, but it would sure look good when we meet with everyone tomorrow if they could see your journal writing was up to date." When I roll my eyes, she gives up. "Never mind, Amber, go do your thing. After I journal, I'm going to take a hot soak in the tub and forget about it all." That's easy for her to say. This dumb conference will decide my whole life, but no worries, right?

Mom makes her way up to her room to scribble down her feelings, while I toss the pizza box in the trash and clean up the kitchen. Then I head back up to my room with a mixture of dread and anticipation.

I'm staring at the dark screen of the computer, which is in sleep mode. I'm working the nerve up to click it on. "Crap! Let's do this!" I say aloud. Anything is better than not knowing. I watch the site come up…I see my dad's smiling portrait and… nothing more. I decide to pull up Facebook's own Missing Persons page, scrolling down until I find where Thomas Wilcox has been added in along with all the other names of missing people. Each one has a picture and a statement telling when they went missing. Mothers and fathers, sisters and brothers, little kids, even old people, all disappeared. Pictures showing some smiling like they hadn't a care in the world, others just staring vacantly into the camera lens. Goosebumps are crawling up my arms. I have seen enough. With a shudder, I switch the computer off.

I wander around my room looking for my sketchpad and that Feelings Journal. I start writing down some stuff about feeling overwhelmed and sad that the world can be such a disappointment to a lot of people, including myself. I wonder what we are all doing here, spinning around in space. Are we all alone in the universe, and does anyone or anything give a care about any of us? Feeling really bummed with these depressed thoughts, I slam the notebook shut and toss it down to the end of the bed.

I start drawing in my sketchpad, trying to lift my mood up: a field of sunflowers swaying in the wind, with big puffy clouds, and the sun peeking out from behind them. Then I start one of a little kid holding hands with her mom and dad, walking in the park imagining they will go feed some ducks or something.

Feeling calmer, I get up and start picking out clothes for tomorrow's possible doomsday. What should I wear for possibly the last day of my school life? I suppose I better pick something halfway decent to look like a good kid. This is kind of hard, on account of the fact that I am no fashion expert. After scattering half the clothes I own all over my bed, I finally decide on a black knit sweater, a colorful scarf, and my best pair of boyfriend jeans.

I am ready to call it a day. I go out in the hall to see if my mom is out of the bathroom. Seeing the coast clear, I go in to brush my teeth, rinse my makeup off and climb into pajamas. Back in my room, I crawl into bed and hope sleep will find me fast.

Chapter Fifteen

MY LOUD ALARM goes off, which is always bad enough, until I remember that it's a terrible day to be me. Feeling like it's doomsday, I groan and throw off my two blankets and one bedspread. I could care less about showering. I just get dressed and stomp downstairs, and then slump into the hard kitchen chair. Since Mom is still busy getting ready, I put my head down on the table and try to go back to sleep. My head is throbbing with anxiety and my mouth is dry. I get up and pour some orange juice to drink, but now there's a lump in my throat and I can barely swallow anything. I put my head back down onto the table to shut out the world. The next minute Mom puts a hand on my shoulder, saying it's time to go. I make myself get up and out to the car, dragging my backpack behind me on the still unshoveled sidewalk. This irritates my mother.

"Amber," she says sharply, "you're not two years old, and it's not the end of the world. Your book bag is getting all wet.

You'll ruin it if you're not careful, and I can't get another one until next year."

I let her babble on about having no extra money to waste and tune her out. The drive, which is normally fifteen minutes, is now turning into twenty-five minutes as we find ourselves in stalled traffic due to heavy rain that is fast turning into sleet. Every mom on the planet is on the road, driving their kid to school. She finally gets there and finds a place to park. We jump out and she starts hurrying me along to get inside. In spite of how crummy it is outside, I plod along, making her mad again. She tells me it's not my last day on earth and to hurry up. As we shove our way through the front doors with a bunch of other loud, wet-smelling kids, she says, "I promise, you will make it through this." She takes my arm and pulls me down the hall. We duck into the guidance office and shut out all the boisterous sounds of slamming lockers and kids shouting to each other from the hallway.

My head is definitely pounding now, and I feel nauseous. We enter a tiny conference room to see the team of my teachers and guidance counselor already seated around a long table that barely fits inside the room. All eyes are on us as we take two empty seats closest to the door. There is one chair left unoccupied. I hope Dr. Bug Eyes remembers to show up.

Mrs. Savage nods unsmilingly at my mom and doesn't even spare me a glance. She looks instead at the clock and announces that we should get started without Dr. Jenkins, because we need to stay on schedule.

"Perhaps Dr. Jenkins has been delayed by the weather. However, we can fill him in with our findings at some point."

Her eyes glitter like polished little stones as she finally zeros in on me.

"Your teachers and I agree that while some progress has been made in raising your grades, you still refuse to modify your behavior, Amber. Your refusal to accept responsibility for your aggressive actions, together with your part in engaging in physical conflicts with other students, has placed us in the position of having to decide what's best for your own safety and that of our student population." She then swivels her head to face my mother. "In other words, the team feels that some period of suspension is advisable at this time. Mr. Wayne is also in agreement with this decision."

My mother is turning a brick-red color, and she's gripping the edges of the table so hard it's turning her knuckles white. I have never seen her so angry. She opens her mouth to reply, but is interrupted by the voice of Dr. Jenkins, giving a cheery good morning to us all.

"I'm so sorry to be joining you late," he continues as he slides smoothly into the seat next to mine, "but there was an accident that slowed traffic coming across town." He starts distributing packets to the entire team. "I have here some copies of current assignments I have Amber working on, such as her Feelings Journal, as we call it. As you know, we have been working on strategies to reduce her anxieties, which have caused her to act out in times past. It is my considered opinion that she is working in good faith to correct these unhealthy tendencies and has made much progress toward her goal of keeping her temper under control. On page one you will see the specific strategies I have taught her to calm herself during stressful situations both in and out of school. Page two shows her reflections about how these are working out for her." He pauses to note the effect this new information has on the team. They are engrossed in reading the documents in front of them.

Mrs. Savage reluctantly applies herself to her packet too. There is silence for a few minutes as everyone reads his findings. Mr. Bug Eyes could possibly be the hero here, even though he sure doesn't remotely look like a knight in shining armor to me!

Mom and I glance at each other, hardly daring to breathe. Now some of the teachers are nodding in agreement at what they're reading. Mrs. Savage notes this, which forces her to call for a vote to determine if they are all willing to continue to work with me. It's unanimous—Dr. Jenkins has won them over, as long as Principal Wayne signs off on it.

"A lot will depend on your attitude, Amber. Let's not forget that, not for a minute," Mrs. Savage says, looking like she's sucking on a lemon. Her eyes narrow as she looks directly at me. "You must prove and continue to assure your teachers that you really want to get along with everyone on a daily basis. No more fights will be tolerated. If there is even one more altercation with another student, you will automatically be suspended for a period of three weeks. Do you agree to these conditions?"

I take a deep breath and manage to nod my head, which is still throbbing. I meet her stare for stare, even though I feel my face getting very warm.

Dr. Jenkins breaks the spell with an optimistic, "Fine, that is fine, Amber. I know you will keep your promise to everyone here, but especially to yourself! You need to be good to yourself, so let's start the process by having you see yourself in a better light. Promise me you will think about what I have said."

I nod fast, so I can get out of here.

Mom and I exit the claustrophobic room and I double over, exhaling the bad air of the office and then gulping in the fresher air of the hallway. Mom is already halfway down the hall, talking back over her shoulder to me.

"I asked Chloe's mom to pick you up from school since I have to make up more time at work." She catches the dirty look I throw her and stops. "I didn't want you stewing by yourself afterward, because I didn't know how things would turn out. I will pick you up by six from their house." She disappears around the corner, leaving me in no rush to get to the office for a pass for my next class.

The remainder of the day is a blur, until the final bell rings and I am free. I step outside, squinting in the bright winter sun, feeling like a prisoner leaving jail after years on the inside. I hear a honk from across the street and see Chloe's mom with the window rolled down, waving. I make my way over and hop in the back seat, hoping she will get the message not to talk. No such luck.

"Well," she says brightly, peering through the rearview mirror at me, "how did it go today?"

I paste on an upbeat look and say things are great.

Her wrinkled brow soothes in relief. "I am so glad to hear it worked out for you, Amber. I know your mom has been worried sick." She quickly adds, "I know how hard you have worked to make things right." She finally starts the car and heads for her house. "We have a couple of hours before I have to come back for Chloe. There's just a few more days now before the concert. I'm so glad you and your mom will be sitting with me the day of, because I always have a case of the nerves for Chloe before an important concert. The shows never seem to bother her, but I know she will be glad you are there supporting her."

That goes without saying; we always have each other's backs for the big stuff, although I have to admit, Chloe is better at that than I am.

I reassure her mom, since she is glancing back at me for some reply. She smiles and then adds I will have time to get homework done before we get Chloe. We reach their house and go inside. "There's a snack for you on the kitchen counter. Feel free to eat there or take it upstairs to the study and set up next to the computer. I have to start a load of wash." I mumble my thanks, glad that they have this thing called a study/library, where I will be left alone to check my secret account.

I get myself set up, laying out homework stuff in case she comes in unexpectedly. Then, for good measure, I start my breathing exercises and affirmations from the Doc's bag of tricks. I still get nervous when I open up the secret web page, on account of the amount of troll messages I get. Anything from, "Tough luck, he's long gone," to, "He's dead, why don't you follow in his footsteps?"

These creeps think they can say anything and remain anonymous just because I am not good at hacking into their point of origin. I hope there's a special spot that's very hot for this type of bottom feeder. I press my fingers to my temples and start a rolling motion, feeling a headache coming on.

I start scrolling down, not seeing anything but the usual. Will anything ever change in my life? I stare morosely at the screen thinking of how I am still being challenged almost daily by the Gruesome Twosome and their whisper campaigns. They've gotten some minions to pretend they are just trying to help me by letting me know what juicy gossip is being passed around about me. You know the type. I've tried to shake it off by writing furiously in my journal. I draw little daggers or faces of them with long forked tongues, wiggling like the snakes they are. That helps some, but I bet it's not quite what old Dr. Jenkins had in mind!

Later on, we go back and get Chloe home. She's exhausted and not in much mood to talk, other than to raise her eyebrows questioningly and see me shake my head a little, to tell her there's nothing new from the site. Mom comes at six to retrieve me, and I spend another boring evening with her and then another two boring days at school.

Chapter Sixteen

WINTER FEST FINALLY arrives, and Mom and I go with Chloe's family to the school concert. Mom's been working overtime with the activities director at the nursing home, trying to arrange volunteers to come and visit the residents with no family. Old folks get real sad and depressed around the holidays if their families are too far away to visit them. Many of them have had their friends die on them too, so they are truly alone during the holidays. I sure don't ever want to get old; things are bad enough for me now!

My mind drifts along, almost tuning out the usual favorites Chloe and the choir always sing, but now they are starting a piece from Handel's Messiah. I am totally getting pulled into it, like riding the crest of a huge wave. Surging sounds pour out, every voice singing in perfect harmony. Mom catches my amazed expression and looks pleased that I'm actually into it. She grins and I feel myself smiling back.

The concert ends with "Let There Be Peace on Earth," and the audience is up on their feet with thunderous appreciation.

"Fantastic concert! All Chloe's hard work really paid off!" Mom congratulates Chloe's proud family. Everybody is grabbing their stuff and filling up the aisles as fast as they can to head out. We are swept along with them, and then we fight our way to a back hall room where the choir is changing out of their robes and back into street clothes. Mom and Chloe's dad and little brother wait there, while Chloe's mom and I shove inside. It's so hot under the stage lights that lots of kids just wear the bare minimum under their robes, so they don't faint dead away. Some moms are fanning their darlings or running to get their water bottles. I spy Chloe and she bounces over to us, beaming, not one frizzy hair on her head.

"I'm starving," she states, which makes her mom and me laugh. "Let's try for Chipotle." Chloe's parents have picked us up in their Lexus RX, which is fine by me. I don't have to listen to Mom overreact to every snowflake on the road.

Inside the restaurant, we join a long line of other -concert-goers with the same idea. Now I suddenly become aware of wild snorting and snickering going on further down the line from us. I peek over my shoulder to find the source and yep, sure enough, the mean girl Gruesome Twosome are back there and have spotted us. I roll my eyes hard and nudge Chloe. "Don't look now, but guess who's back there? Just our luck."

Chloe wrinkles her nose up as if she smells something really bad. "Don't give them the satisfaction, Amber. Just ignore them and stay cool." We all place our orders, look around, and finally spot a table. Our moms are oblivious to everything, as are Chloe's dad and brother, who are too busy talking sports to notice these two flouncing past laughing their "mean girl" screechy laughs. They really should try and bottle that sound so they won't have to work so hard at producing the high-pitched screechiness. They take seats diagonally across from us. Their moms are oblivious too, evidently. How can parents be so blind to what their darlings do right under their noses?

Chloe remains unruffled by the stage whispers, even though she can hear what they are saying, because her seat is closer to them. "Chloe sounded real good with her solo tonight. Too bad she's still stuck with that loser friend of hers," Miss Devious says.

"Yeah, she sticks to her like a loser leech would stick to your skin and suck all the blood out of you," adds Miss Deception.

"Well, you know that she is a pity friend. Chloe feels sorry for her, that's the reason why," says Kelly, A.K.A. Miss Devious. With that she gets up from her seat laughing her hyena laugh and meanders toward our table, walking backwards. Her laugh continues to grate on my nerves so much that before I know it, my foot develops a mind of its own. It inches out into the aisle, where she stumbles over it. She flings her arm out to catch herself and catches my arm instead.

"You did that on purpose, Amber," she shrieks, pulling her arm back quick as if she had touched a hot stove, and glares in my face.

"It was on accident," I counter, "just like when you whipped your backpack into the back of my head a couple of weeks ago, remember?"

The adults at both tables—and actually more than a few tables—swivel their heads around with their mouths hanging open.

Finally, my mom sputters, "I'm sure Amber didn't mean to trip you, dear. It is very crowded in here, after all." Miss Devious narrows her eyes at me again and stomps off to the rest room.

Entertainment over, restaurant talk goes back to normal and I am forgotten, except for the looks I am getting from the Gruesome Twosome's moms. They whisper away while staring at me. Then in unison, they push back their chairs and start marching over to our table. Casey follows with a self-righteous look on her face.

Kelly's mom pipes up in a snotty voice, "You need to monitor your daughter's behavior better; she definitely tripped my daughter just now." Miss Deception's mom chimes in. "Yes, Amber's actions have caused a great deal of problems for my daughter too," she says haughtily. "We know she has been suspended because of her bad temper."

"Really?" my mom snaps back. "It seems to me that Amber is not operating in a vacuum here, but rather reacting to the intimidating and underhanded behavior initiated by both of your daughters!"

"Your daughter uses violence as a means to an end," says Casey's mom through clenched teeth.

Mom slowly pushes her chair back and stands up, her hands on her hips. Meanwhile, Chloe's mom and dad and brother's necks swivel from one combatant to the other, like they are watching a tennis match.

"Amber is learning coping strategies from her therapist, whom she had to start seeing because of the bullying tactics from your two girls. It seems they could do with some monitoring from you too."

"What you really mean is that your kid can't control her violent tendencies, so that our girls have to use their words to defend themselves." Now all three moms have their hands on their hips, making me wish the ground would open up and swallow us all up. Casey is sneering and Kelly, who has gotten back from the restroom, comes over to stand next to her mom, automatically mimicking her aggressive body language.

Chloe's dad clears his throat noisily; he has noticed we are attracting unwanted attention again.

"Maybe now is not the time or the place to have this conversation, ladies," he says, clearing his throat again nervously.

Chloe, who is sitting perfectly still, not saying boo, suddenly springs up, projecting her voice like she has been taught in the choir. "I have something to say and I think it will solve this problem for good." She leans down to grab her book bag, into which she'd jammed her choir robe to save time getting to the concert, and unzips it fast. She pulls out her binder and rips out six sheets of paper.

"What's with all the paper, Chloe?" I am feeling exhausted and embarrassed now and just want to get home. All the moms are looking just as exasperated. Kelly's mom taps her foot impatiently.

"Just bear with me for two minutes. Each of you will get one sheet of paper and crumple it up, but don't rip it. I saw this taught in an actual classroom situation on YouTube recently in an assignment for my humanities class." She is standing up and handing out sheets. "Remember, crumple the paper up as hard as you can, but don't shred it." All three moms and myself, plus Kelly and Casey, look at each other frowning, then start wadding up the paper hard and tight into a small ball.

"Okay, now unfold it carefully and throw it on the floor here. Start stepping on it and dragging it around to get it smudged and dirty. Now pick it up and notice the effects of the wrinkling, stomping and smashing." Everybody does what she asks, still looking annoyed.

"The smashed and dirty paper stands for what happens to all of us through the years as we go through life accumulating hurts and disappointments. The mean stuff we hear about ourselves makes us more prone to hard feelings we keep inside. No one is immune to the bad stuff that happens in life. But do we have to inflict more pain by taking cheap shots at each other? This is the Christmas and Hanukkah season. We just sang about peace on earth. It's possible to work together right now to help heal us all and let go of the nasty stuff. Right?"

Chloe looks at Casey and Kelly, next at me, and then all the moms.

"Why not promise here and now to make the commitment to do better and change the future for all of us today, okay?" she pleads.

We all stare at the floor and then start sneaking looks at each other.

Chloe speaks directly to Kelly. "We were friends in grade school until you thought I was replacing you with Amber. Then Casey was friends with you and me, and Amber felt left out.

Guys, this was years back and we are a lot older now. We can move past this and be respectful of each other, even if we aren't best friends now. Will you give it a try?"

Kelly shuffles her foot back and forth, thinking. Finally she says, "Well, I never had a problem with you, Chloe, and yeah, maybe I was jealous of Amber, but like you say, we are all older now, so I guess we can all move on from this." She looks at Casey and asks, "What do you think?"

Casey nods her head. "Okay by me."

Now we swivel our heads in unison to our moms. They all look at each other silently. Then Mom says, "Truce?" They all smile half-heartedly and promise to stop feuding.

Chloe's parents look relieved and start gathering up their belongings.

"Wonderful!" Her dad jovially wishes us all a great holiday. Almost all the crowd has cleared out, and we head out quickly. Just one more school day tomorrow and I won't have to think of those girls or their moms for two glorious weeks.

OUR LAST DAY goes off without a hitch. Both the students and teachers are in a good mood all day, with kids slamming lockers and yelling, "See you after break!" texting on their cell phones up to the last minute. Then the final bell rings and we race out breathing in the cold air and pile onto buses or into cars leaving those classrooms behind. Hallelujah and good riddance to it all!

Chapter Seventeen

CHRISTMAS IS FOUR days away and it's snowing hard. In the past couple years, we would only have a light dusting of the white stuff, but when I woke up this morning, it was already sticking. Weather reports called for continued accumulation of up to five inches throughout the day. I'm hypnotized by it coming down in chunks and swirling around the tiny front yard. I am on my own today, as Mom had to make her way to work in spite of the snow.

Last night at dinner, we almost got into a fight over what I want for Christmas: seeing my dad walk through the door. I was honest with her about finding Dad one way or another and insisted she had to know something more than what she's already said. I close my eyes now against the snow whipping around the condo and try to blot out the incessant howling wind, remembering last night's even noisier conversation.

"Amber, I wish you would just realize that he is gone for good, and that is not going to change, no matter how much we would like it to be different. Even your dad's best buddy, a fellow trombone player, couldn't understand how your dad would disappear without a word to anyone, but he did. I wish I could magically make him reappear for you for Christmas, but it is impossible." There were tears of anger and frustration coming down her face.

"Wait, what? What friend? You never mentioned him before. What's his name? Have you got his phone number? I want to talk to him. He might know something, even though he thinks he doesn't. Let's call him right now!"

"Amber, that's crazy. It's eleven o'clock at night. I need to get to bed; I have to do this thing called work tomorrow morning. I shouldn't have let you talk me into watching *It's A Wonderful Life*."

Then I got teary-eyed. "We always watch it every year—it's been our tradition," I sputtered. I had watched this movie with her since I was eight years old. Mom would make hot cocoa and we would curl up on the couch watching Clarence the angel help Jimmy Stewart, who plays George Bailey, understand his importance to friends and his family. He thought life wasn't worth living after he lost all his money and thought he might end up in jail. He wished he'd never been born, then found out how awful things would have turned out if his wish had been granted. The movie represented hope that things happened for a reason, and everything could be better, if we would only trust that good outweighs the bad in the end. How could she not believe this anymore? Life was wearing her down and making me wonder what my life would look like when I reached her advanced age. I started feeling desperate.

"Tell me this guy's name, Mom. I need to follow up every clue possible. Tell me! Now!" I demanded.

"Okay! His name is Mike Hanover, for all the good it will do you. We haven't been in touch for years. He used to send a Christmas card, for the first few years after your dad left. Just remember, your dad and I had already divorced. There was no real reason for Mike to stay in touch after it was evident your dad had disappeared for good."

"Great!" I ignored her lack of motivation. "Give me his cell number, Mom." She rolled her eyes and pulled herself up from the couch to go to her address book in the planning desk.

"Here, have at it; but at least wait until tomorrow. I'm going up to bed. He probably left town a long time ago, like your dad. Musicians have to go where the work is, you know. His number has probably been disconnected years back." She handed her ancient address book over to me and made her way upstairs. "Good night, sweetie. Don't stay up much longer."

Now I'm having second thoughts about whether I should even try calling this so-called best buddy of Dad's. What if he had up and left too? Like Mom said, it's been years. I turn the paper with the number I copied onto it over and over in my hands. Doubts are popping up like weeds. I yank them out of my mind and about-face to get my cell phone. I dial the number and hold my breath.

"The number you have dialed has been disconnected or is no longer in service. Please check the number and dial again," intones a robotic voice.

"Terrific." I start ripping up the paper. "Thanks for nothing, Mike Hanover."

Breathe in through the nose for a count of four, and breathe out slowly through the mouth. Breathe in, expand the diaphragm, and breathe out for another count of four. Dr. Jenkins said it is even used as a Navy SEAL strategy, for staying calm in emergencies. He is always trying to find new ways to convince me to practice my breathing. I don't know if I believe him about the Navy SEALs story, though. Anyway, he says that breathing deeply sends needed oxygen to the brain to allow it to process information better. I should try it and not knock it. I have finally gotten a lot better at this, with practice.

WAIT! A light bulb moment is occurring, maybe because of the oxygen from the deep breathing. The older generation love Facebook, right? Just because Dad wasn't on it doesn't mean this Mike isn't. I race to the computer and bring it out of sleep mode. I plug his name into Facebook's search bar. Wham, about five Mike Hanovers show up. I send out PMs to all five, asking if any know Thomas Wilcox. I tell them that I am his daughter and I am trying to locate him. I direct them to the site I have set up and insist that they answer the questions I put up. Not looking for trolls or perverts, just honest descriptions and answers. I finish my typing and lean back in my chair. I'm feeling frustrated that I will have wait until tomorrow to tell Chloe what I am doing.

For now, I drag myself up and out of the chair and plod upstairs to bed.

Chapter Eighteen

MORNING LIGHT REACHES my eyes early because there are no blackout curtains to keep it out. I sit up in bed, listening to Mom running the shower and getting ready for work. I remember what I must do today, which makes me hop out of bed fast. It's only 7:00, so I have to wait to call Chloe for advice. I throw on jeans and a sweatshirt and look around for warm socks. The icy floor sends goose bumps up my legs…ugh! Finally armed with woolen socks and fluffy slippers, I am ready to go downstairs and turn up the heat.

Breakfast is some quickly made toast and hot cocoa. Then I settle in the swivel chair by the computer and get ready to check for any PMs from complete strangers on Facebook, all Mike Hanovers I found last night.

Mom drags herself into the kitchen, going right past me mumbling about where she left her car keys. She finds them on the kitchen counter where she left the unopened mail from yesterday. I hear her complain about several bills that are coming due soon, and then the cupboards start banging as she looks for a clean coffee cup and cereal bowl. Then there's sudden silence. I feel her coming up behind my chair and realize she is reading the name on my screen as she breathes down my neck.

"What are you doing on this guy's Facebook page, Amber? We don't know this guy from Adam."

"Oh," I say innocently. "I thought this was the right Mike Hanover to get in touch with. The phone number you gave me last night for him is disconnected."

"Amber, I told you that was most likely a dead end."

"Okay, you can save me some more time then and quickly look at these Mike Hanovers before you leave for work. You know what he looks like, so help me check out these pictures."

"This is such a lost cause. Stop wasting your life on this, Amber. He is not the one." I quickly pull up another Mike picture.

"No and no!" she says, her voice ratcheting up two more notches. "Just stop already, will you?"

"There are only a couple more left," I plead, as she turns impatiently away. "Is this the guy?"

"Not him, now stop," as I pull up the fourth one.

"No," she snaps, patience gone. "Why do you keep insist…" And then she stops suddenly. "Wait. Go back to that last one. Let me see that again." I hold my breath, hoping. We both stare at the last Mike's face intently.

A pleasantly smiling man stands in front of a trombone hooked jauntily on top of its stand. He is looking straight at us.

The trombone stand is off to one side and a little behind him, so we both missed it at first glance.

"Well, I'll be a monkey's aunt," she says. "It sure looks like it could be him, except for the gray hairs, but with the trombone there, it means it must be him." She stares, entranced. "I suppose I could get in touch with him, but what good would that do? Just bring back a lot of sad memories." She turns resolutely away. "I have to leave a little early for work, so I've got to get going now."

I don't want to clue her in to what I've already done, so I let her give me a quick peck on the cheek while asking if Chloe can come and hang out. Her mom just works half days at the Y. She could drop Chloe off at our house and then after lunch, she could pick us both up.

"I suppose, if it's okay with Carol. Call me and let me know for sure."

"Will do," I confirm. She leaves, letting a blast of cold air in. I shiver but not just from that. I'm jittery from wondering if and when Mike Hanover will message me back. If he doesn't, I will show up on his doorstep, no matter what.

I get in touch with Carol, Chloe's mom, right away, and she says yes to dropping her off. Chloe says she has no time to shower and that I owe her one. "Just bring your makeup bag and shower when you get here," I say excitedly. "I can't wait to show you what I found!"

A little before 8:30 I hear a car door slam and peek through the curtains to see if it's Chloe. I see her hopping up the steps and hurry to let her in.

"So, what is so important that it couldn't wait till I got my shower?" she huffs, still out of breath and frazzled for having to race around her house to be ready for her mom to drop her off here in time for work.

I drag her over to the computer to show her Mike Hanover's Facebook profile.

She notices the trombone right away; her eyes go wide and then narrow down to a squint. Troubled now, she turns to me for explanation. "This does not look like your dad at all, Amber."

"My who?? No, it's his best friend that Mom told me about over the weekend."

"OMG!" she squeals. "How did you get her to do that?"

"The usual—a combination of teary looks and nagging at her until she was completely worn down. That and letting her know I will not be giving up anytime soon. She gave me her old address book and wished me luck. I looked at all her old stuff in there to see if there was anything else helpful, but I didn't recognize any other people in it. Most had lines crossed through the phone numbers, including Mike's name. I tried it anyway, but only got a recording that it was disconnected. Then I checked Facebook for any central Ohio Mike Hanovers and sent private messages to all five of them. She identified the trombone guy this morning as the right one. Now all I have to do is…"

PING—the notification sound goes off, and I suck in my breath while clicking on it.

From Messenger: *Hi, this is Mike Hanover, Amber. I knew your dad way back when. So amazing at how you have grown up so fast; this is such a blast from the past! Your mom probably told you that we looked everywhere for your dad and even filed a missing person report when he first disappeared. We called hospitals in Columbus, checked his apartment, and went to the jazz places he always played at. Your mom told me he wanted to get back together and for her to meet him where they first met, at the Symphony Hotel Jazz Lounge in Cincinnati. He never showed up at the appointed time. That's all I know, but feel free to call me at 614-364-8841, and we can talk anyway.*

"Amber, this is incredible. This guy sounds legit!" She looks at me and sees I'm hiding my head in my hands and shaking. She puts her hand on my shoulder and gently rubs it. "It's too much to take in all at once," she says softly. "We should probably slow down, get something to drink and relax in the kitchen. Maybe get a snack or something too. Then we can plan your response and how you want to handle this." She leads me still teary-eyed into the kitchen and pushes me into a chair. "Want some chai tea?" She rummages through the closet and pulls out a chai latte K cup, plus some cocoa for herself.

I put my head onto the table and close my eyes while she gets the drinks ready. "Want any munchies?" I mumble "no thanks" as she curls my hand around the hot mug. I force myself to sit up.

Chloe plops down opposite me and asks cheerfully, "Well, are you going to pick up your cell and call this Mr. Hanover or not? After all, you have come this far, you might as well listen to what he has to say."

"I suppose so," I grudgingly agree. "But Mom doesn't want me to do this; she just turned around and left."

"She left it up to you, since she knows she can't really stop you. It's your decision, Amber." She shrugs and leans back in her seat. "But if I know you, and you know I do, you will probably kick yourself if you let this opportunity slip away."

I sip some tea, tapping my fingers on the side of the mug. "Let's do this," I say, "and let whatever happens, happen." I punch in the number and put it on speaker, so Chloe can hear too.

We hear it ring a few times and then he picks up. "Hello? This is Mike Hanover. Is this Amber?"

My throat is dry, but I make myself answer, "Yes, hi." My voice comes out like a frog's croak, so I try again, "Yes, hi, Mr. Hanover, this is Thomas Wilcox's daughter and I am trying to locate my dad. I got the text you privately messaged me. I want to ask you some more questions. Maybe you can remember something else that would hopefully point me in the right direction."

"Oh, I'm so sorry, Amber. I wish I could help more, I really do! I told you about all that your mom and I did in searching for him. And the police were no help at all, since they said he probably just decided to not show up where he said he would meet your mom that day. He lived in Columbus, not too far from me, so we checked there and at the hospitals, in case something had happened to him. We even checked with the state highway patrol that day, to make sure he wasn't in an accident getting there, but there was nothing. We also put flyers up around the city in places that he tended to go. I think he must have gotten cold feet and could not bring himself to start over with your mom. They had already been divorced by that time, you know."

Yes, I do know and I wish people would stop reminding me of it! "What about his playing? He wouldn't just give that up, right? He had to eat and pay bills, so how could he up and leave the area he worked in for so long? There has to be more to this. How did he find jobs anyway?" My head is aching and I know I'm going to break down crying any minute now.

Mike is quiet as if considering my last question. Finally he says, "We were well known in town by word of mouth and would substitute for the Columbus Symphony Orchestra every once in a great while. But your dad's heart was set on playing jazz. Of course, we both paid to have our names and addresses placed in what's called *The Local Musicians Directory for Central Ohio.* Musicians from all over Ohio can pay to put their names and addresses in if they work freelance or have full- or part-time jobs. We all pay union dues to contract for living wages, instead of having to be at the mercy of employers. Names are renewed annually, but his was never renewed after the year he went missing."

My ears perk up on the last bit of his story and I feel my heart lurch. "Has anyone checked for him in that directory lately?"

"Well, ah…no, but since I haven't bumped into him in these last ten years, I would say that would be a dead end. I checked each year for the first few years after he went missing." My whole body slumps in dejection as he speaks kindly, but with finality.

"How's your mom these days, Amber? I regret us losing touch and hope you will give her my regards. I hope some day we will find out what happened to your dad, because we were buddies for years. I have no clue why he didn't at least try to call one of us and let us know he was okay. People can be funny like that; you think you know someone but..." He lets his voice fade away.

Tears are streaming down my face and I am losing it. "Mr. Hanover, would you please just check one more time in your Local Union Directory? Please? And then I promise I will leave you alone. I can't let it go until I hear you say it's not there, once and for all."

Chloe has tears in her eyes now too and is patting my hand frantically.

"Amber, I, well, okay, hold on, I have to dig for it; it's sort of messy around here, bear with me." We hear him yanking open desk drawers and slamming them shut. Finally, he lays his hands on it.

"Okay, got it, it's the latest one." He shuffles through the pages to the end, breathing noisily. I hold my own breath and Chloe holds tightly to my hand, biting her lip.

Dead silence is all we hear now. It stretches on forever and is deafening to me. I am chewing my own lip so hard that I taste blood.

Then we hear him shout, "No way, no crazy way!"

I yell back, "Mike, Mike, what's going on?" The heck with formalities now!

"Oh, heaven above, I can't believe it; this can't be happening. It's here! Your dad's name and current address are right here! Let me double-check the date on this directory...yes, it's the latest one. Amber, he's in here with an email address, street address, and cell number!"

Chapter Nineteen

CHLOE AND I look at each other, dumbfounded. It's too much to take in all at once. Have I really just found my dad? Is it possible it was that easy? Has he been here the whole time? No, Mike said he looked for a few years, but with no luck. To think if I hadn't been my usual stubborn self, I might never have made this discovery.

So now, all I have to do is call his cell and say, *"Where the hell have you been all these years!"* My face is flushed and I am about to hyperventilate. *No deep breathing, sorry, Dr. Jenkins.* There are times in life when you just can't breathe slowly. Chloe is hardly daring to breathe at all. I can tell she is holding it.

"Don't faint on me, Chloe, I need you!" I plead, desperate for her support. I can see her visibly make an effort to pull herself together.

What now? She mouths the words to me, but I'm not sure how to answer.

"Mike, are you still there? I need his cell number and street address from you. Then I have to hang up and call my dad right away."

"Wait, Amber, that may not be the best idea. Let me call him first. If he hasn't even bothered to tell me he is back, then you might scare him off, if you called suddenly like that. He could shut you and your mom out completely. And he doesn't live close by; he lives in Logan, near the Hocking Hills area. I will get back to you ASAP. Even if he's not home, I will at least let you know for sure." His voice has a pleading tone. "We don't want him disappearing on us again, right? Does this sound like a plan you can live with?"

I want answers fast but am trying to see his point. "Okay, I will try it your way, but I need to hear something back fast. My friend's mom is coming to pick us up at noon." I glance at the clock. "That's just forty minutes from now."

"Then I will call now," he says and disconnects.

Chloe and I look at each other. "Did that conversation just happen or am I in an alternate universe right now?" I try to joke, but my face is hot and feels blotchy. I touch my neck and realize I am breaking out in hives! Chloe notices and gets some paper towels, which she wets down and hands to me. I start patting at my hot skin with shaky hands. Then I glance at the clock and frown. Chloe gathers up her tote bag and down jacket.

"So much for that shower," she says. I keep my cell handy while looking for my bag and jacket. It's not made from down, so I take a scarf and ski cap, plus alpaca mittens, which is the one luxury item Mom can afford for this winter.

We wait by the door. I'm worrying about hearing back from Mike before Carol shows up.

Chapter Twenty

AFTER A WHILE, Chloe notices a car driving slowly down the slippery street.

"Amber, I think I see my mom," she says.

I hear my cell ringing and I punch up the call. "Hello, Mike?"

"Yeah, hi, Amber." He sounds somber. "Your dad didn't answer, so I just want to let you know that I will keep calling. I also left a voicemail. If he doesn't get back to me in, say, an hour, I will call again and keep at it until he does."

My voice wavers as I respond. "Okay, Mike. Thanks so much for trying. My friend's mom is about to pull into my driveway so I will talk to you soon. Thanks again for everything you are doing!"

We hustle down the steps and hop into Carol's car.

"Hi girls, how was your morning?" she asks.

"Fine." Chloe pastes on a smile, but I sink down into the seat. I'm feeling wiped out, and it's only a little past noon.

"What do you feel like for lunch, ladies? Your choices are St. Louis Panera Bread restaurant or Five Guys. I know Amber likes French fries and we can get them at Five Guys. We can indulge once in a while, Chloe," she jokes. She looks in the mirror at us and sees the way I am slouching. "Everything okay, girls?" Her Mom radar starts pinging.

"It's all good, Mom, really." Chloe nudges me and I struggle to sit up.

"Panera Bread is fine," I answer. "I can get carbs from the broccoli cheddar soup and then be healthy with a half salad." I try to sound upbeat as her mom heads toward the Mill Run area.

"Panera it is then," Carol agrees.

The place is packed, and once more we are in a long line. I check behind us to make sure there is no repeat of finding Kelly and Casey. Then I would really wonder if I'm in an alternate universe! There are no surprises, however, as we wait for our turn, so I start relaxing. Chloe is uncharacteristically fidgety and Carol notices. "You girls seem uptight, as if you are waiting for the proverbial shoe to drop. Anything wrong?"

"Nothing, Mom," Chloe reassures her. "Just starved is all." She forces another smile. Carol's attention is pulled back to the cashier, who asks if she has a My Panera card and that is the end of it. The cashier gives us cups and a pager and we start hunting up a booth or table. We finally find a spot way in the back and settle in, waiting for the pager to buzz.

Carol makes small talk about the weather and how close to Christmas it's getting. She says she's still shopping for last-minute gifts and that she feels under pressure to cook a big holiday dinner. Chloe's aunts and uncles and four little cousins are coming, plus her family always invites both sets of grandparents. I wonder idly what it would feel like to sit around a table set for sixteen, with everyone talking at once. I picture the excitement from the little kids in awe of a tree surrounded by presents. Would everyone open all their gifts at once or would they take turns, so they could admire each gift? Chloe's extended family is musical like she is, and she has remarked in years past how they all sit around the piano afterwards and sing Christmas carols. I let out a dejected sigh, wishing for just one Christmas with my dad. A traitorous tear seeps from the corner of my eye and I dab at it, hoping no one notices.

The jarring sound of the pager wakes me from this daydream, and we jump up to collect our food. We march back to our seats and start eating. My food tastes like sawdust, and I see Chloe pushing her salad around her bowl.

"You girls are certainly quiet," Carol remarks. "Anything I should know about or maybe help you with?"

I moisten my lips; they feel like sandpaper. I dig in my bag for my lip balm to give myself time to think of an answer. Chloe looks to me for a clue as to how to set the tone of the conversation.

I find myself saying, "I am especially missing my dad for some reason this year." So true, but how much more to divulge? "Mom wishes I would forget about him, but that's not going to happen. I will always wonder what happened. Mom told me he died in Afghanistan, but I found out that's not true. He is still alive, and I told her that I'm going to find him, one way or another."

There, the elephant is now out in the room and flipping somersaults!

Carol's eyebrows rise up to her bangs. "Wow! What does she say to that idea?"

"She stopped throwing up roadblocks, but she isn't exactly helping either," I say.

"Okay, well, what have you done so far in searching for him, unless you'd rather not say? There are many people looking for their disappeared loved ones, whether they are adopted or like you, Amber, with someone out there they are wishing they could find. Actually, there are websites to help you in locating missing people." She looks thoughtfully at me. "How far have you gotten in your search?"

My mouth erupts like an unstoppable lava flow. "Chloe helped me set up a website to direct people to that may have known my dad or might know of where he is currently. We put up questions for them to answer to prove they are who they say they are. So far, all I've gotten have been visits by trolls—those are the ones that go from website to website commenting nasty stuff on all of them," I add, in case she doesn't know who trolls are and what they do. "There were plenty of those types of comments, saying hateful things about Dad and myself." My eyes tear up remembering some of the nastier replies.

Carol's eyebrows are getting a workout. She looks from her daughter to me and then to her daughter again. "When did you learn how to do all that?"

"It's all taught in my computer literacy class." Chloe shrugs. Since Chloe is a talented and gifted student, she is allowed several electives, not normally open to our age group, like the humanities class where she researched her project on the hurtful things people do to each other.

She takes herself out of the hot seat by focusing on me. "Amber is amazing in her determination. She called up her dad's best friend, after her mom let his name slip. She found him on Facebook and sent a private message. He gave her his cell number, said he would help, and checked some musicians' business directory for her dad's current address and—"

"Mike thinks he may have found my dad in the current directory for central Ohio," I add.

Carol's jaw drops and her fork slips through her fingers to clatter onto her plate.

"You just called this stranger up?" Her voice is low but horrified. "How would you know he was the real deal?"

I hasten to reassure her. "Mom identified him on his profile but advised me not to contact him. She said they had lost touch, and we were off his radar many years ago, and so not to bother." I don't mention that I contacted all the Mike Hanovers in the Columbus metro area and showed her their pictures after the fact.

"Wow," she says in a hushed tone. "Does your mom know about this?"

"Nope; it just happened before you picked us up for lunch. She'd already left for work."

"And you say this Mr. Hanover is calling your dad to see if it is really him, after all this time? Amber, you need to tell her about all this. It wouldn't be right keeping this secret. I am certainly glad you're telling me now," and here she glances in Chloe's direction, with a look that says they will be having a little talk later, "but if you don't include your mom, you are asking for real trouble down the road. You should tell her tonight, okay?" she pleads.

Grudgingly, I agree. I dread the scene that's coming in just a few hours.

Chapter Twenty-One

WE FINISH UP our lunch with little left to say. Carol says she needs to make a quick stop at the library to drop off overdue books and look for new ones.

"We'll hang out there for a while before going back to our house," she decides. "We're all feeling on edge, so maybe some down time at the library will help us relax." We pull into the library parking lot and pick up the pace to get inside. The wind is bitterly cold. I remember wondering not long ago if my dad was homeless somewhere, and I'm glad I found that's not the case. I wish everyone could be in a warm, cheerful place for the holidays.

Carol says she will meet us in the lobby in about half an hour, give or take. She leaves us to ourselves and I start thinking maybe we could hunt up this directory Mike has. We head over to the information desk and inquire. The librarian says no, that is a private directory and not held in a public library. I shrug off my disappointment and we decide to hang out in one of the small study rooms until it's time to meet up in the lobby. We hand over our library cards to the librarian on duty upstairs and she reserves us a half hour inside a small room.

I grumble to Chloe that I will have to face the music when my mom gets home.

"You aren't the only one, Amber," she reminds me. "Did you catch the look my mom threw my way? I am not looking forward to all her questions either." She looks dejected and I feel guilty for only thinking about myself.

"I sure hope I haven't gotten you into trouble with your mom. I shouldn't have blabbed about the website we made. I'm so sorry, Chloe. Sometimes I wonder how you put up with having me for a friend. Maybe Kelly and Casey are right; I'm a royal pain in the butt."

This puts a rueful smile on Chloe's mouth. "You sure are!" She laughs and jabs me on the elbow. Then her smile disappears. "Too late now," she adds gloomily. "We will both have to face the music tonight. But it's almost Christmas, so maybe our moms will show mercy. Here's hoping, anyway."

"You are always such an optimist about everything. I am the exact opposite, but at least I know now that my dad is still around. I'll just have to focus on that, while Mom is screaming louder than an ambulance siren."

"Christmas is just three days off now," Chloe remarks. "Tell your mom how much you're hoping your dad can be found and how we managed to do exactly that. Actually, all the credit goes to you for accomplishing that by going after Mr. Hanover.

When you make up your mind about getting something done, your focus is sharper than any knife could be." She grins in spite of her annoyance.

"Well, you're the one with the calm, keep-your-chin-up-and-push-through-it-all attitude. Without you staying so cool, I doubt I would have kept trying; I'm too moody and have a bad habit of second-guessing myself about everything I do."

"That's the artist in you, most likely. Better to feel deeply about things than not at all, you know."

"Maybe," I muse, "but I wish I could be calmer about things and get on top of my temper. Do you think people can actually change through the years?" Waves of doubt pound me harder than waves at high tide. "Did he change his mind about wanting to try again with my mom? How can a person watch the years roll by and never try and contact his family?" A scary thought strikes me, making me shiver again, but this time with an icy fear. "What if he has another family after all this time? What if that's why he hasn't bothered to be my dad? Oh, Chloe, I can't bear thinking he might have another family with another daughter who gets to spend each Christmas with him." I start wailing and tears start flowing. "That must be it. Why didn't I ever consider it before? He's got another family by now and won't want to have anything to do with me ever." Even though the study rooms are basically soundproof, my loud voice makes one librarian glance our way with a concerned look.

Chloe shushes me. "Stop it," she snaps. She is worn out and irritated by all my drama. "Stop imagining the worst-case scenarios you can possibly think of, Amber. We know nothing of the kind. It could be something completely different."

"Like what?" I sniffle. "What else could it be? What makes a dad disappear, pay no child support for years and then suddenly reappear, put his name back in the local musicians' directory, like nothing has ever happened?"

"I don't know, maybe he had an accident and lost his memory or something." She sounds exasperated, for once. Chloe looks at the clock and starts pulling on her coat. "I refuse to speculate, and you shouldn't either. Come on, it's time to go downstairs and find my mom." She's definitely mad now.

I brush tears away and mumble an apology. It's bad enough my dad may not want to be a real dad now that I've found him, but it would be worse if my best friend has had it with me too. She throws me a look over her shoulder as we start downstairs. "Oh, stop looking at me like it's the end of the world. Things will turn out for the best, you'll see."

Carol is standing in the lobby frowning and looking around for us. Her look is tense when she spots us and says, "Let's go girls, it's getting late."

We head back out into the nasty weather, where the wind is now pitching a fit of its own. Nobody talks much on the way to Chloe's. Once there, we plop on the couch listlessly, in contrast to her mom's busyness as she goes about straightening things up and checking the pantry for what to make for dinner. "Your dad is picking up your brother at the community center on the way home from work, Chloe. We will probably have chicken tacos for dinner with a salad. Unless you want fish tacos instead."

"Nah, chicken is fine, Mom," she answers flatly.

Carol's cell goes off and she answers, and then tells me it's my mom. "She's on her way over, Amber. She's not feeling well and is leaving work early." She stands in the doorway and gives me a stern look. "Go easy on each other tonight. Best to tell her what you know directly. It's bound to be a shock."

I nod and pick up some magazines I've been sitting on and set them on the coffee table. Her cell rings again and she turns away to answer it.

"I'll text you, Chloe, and keep you in the loop about whatever Mike finds out. That is, if Mom doesn't try to confiscate my cell phone and keep him from calling. If she has it out with him and offends him, I'm afraid of what might happen. He may not want to deal with her or even me, for that matter. So depending on if I feel she is up to hearing about all this, I may not even tell her anything tonight." *Or ever,* I say under my breath. "And again, I'm terribly sorry that I've gotten you into trouble with your mom." I send her an anxious look, to which she responds with a tired smile.

"It will be okay, Amber, trust me. You know my mom; she rarely hits the roof about anything, and when she does, it's never for long."

We hear a car pull into the garage and I see Mom roll into their driveway right behind it. "Got to go," I say.

I receive a weak smile from my best friend. She's distracted by the loud voices of her brother and dad as they come into the house discussing the basketball game, and she turns away from me.

I hear Mom honking so I grab my coat and take off. I start breathing deeply in preparation for whatever lies ahead.

Chapter Twenty-Two

WE ROLL ONTO our street and park in a spot close to our unit. Sometimes we get lucky like that, but not always. My mom hauls herself out and up to our unit, coughing and sneezing. She says she's going to lie down and asks me to make dinner for myself, because she doesn't think she'll be able to eat anything. I say no problem and look at my cell for any messages I may have missed. There's nothing new from Mike Hanover so I start rummaging through the fridge for something quick I can make. Seems like we will have to make a grocery run soon. I poke through the pantry but see nothing but chili beans and baked beans. I open the freezer and find some frozen pizza to bake. Just as the timer goes off, I get a call from Mike.

I keep my voice just above a whisper, to make sure our conversation won't wake Mom. It's hard to allow Mike to tell me what he knows without demanding instant answers. I have to let him tell me what he knows at his own pace, but he's stopping and starting, with crazy long pauses in between each sentence. I feel like reaching through the phone and shaking him to speed things up.

"Amber, your dad did call me back…I don't know what to make of him though…he sounded strange, almost cryptic, not his easygoing self at all. We went round and round the issue of where he has been all this time…but he was vague about everything. I had to work hard to get him to agree to meet me at all. Finally, he agreed to let me come out to his place in Logan…but refused to even meet me halfway."

"Good, I'll come too; when can you pick me up?"

He sighs and says nothing for the longest time. "Amber, remember you promised to let me check things out first. I know your dad from way back and I know something is not right here. Something is way off. Your dad's voice sounds flat and almost robotic, not himself. I am going tomorrow to see him and then I will know the lay of the land and how to advise you on how to approach him. We will come up with a plan as to what to do, okay?" Reluctantly I agree, and he promises to call back after he's seen Dad.

We say goodbye and I open the oven to an overcooked and wilted pizza that tastes no better than the cardboard box it came in. I find I have no appetite anyhow and dump it all in the trash. After pacing around and feeling ready to explode if I don't keep busy, I figure I better eat something. I pull out some Froot Loops cereal. In between crunches, I replay the day in my head. After more second-guessing myself, I'm starting to feel almost feverish. The idea that I might not get to see my dad face-to-face is more than I can bear, so I shoot Mike a text, insisting that he take me with him tomorrow. There's no reply.

My phone screen lights up twenty minutes later. He messages me that he wants to come over to see Mom and me. I chew my lip while texting our address to him. I glance at the time. He says it will be about twenty-five minutes to get here. I say, great, knowing it's not.

I hear the toilet flush, and a minute later Mom comes into the kitchen, coughing and shivering in her flannel pajamas and bathrobe. I offer to make her tea or cocoa and she chooses hot chocolate. She sits and wrinkles her nose. "Smells like burnt pizza. What happened?"

I shrug and say I didn't time it correctly. I hand her the cocoa, which she sips carefully. I don't know how to break the news to her that Mike is coming over in about fifteen more minutes. I start by saying that I did call him and he really wants to come and see us and talk about Dad.

She shakes her head and then puts it down on top of the table, cradling it in her hands. "Well, maybe sometime after the holidays," she says, too exhausted to argue about it.

I clear my throat and say, "The thing is, Mom, um, the thing is he can't wait till then. He's kind of on his way over now." Her face turns ashen; her eyes are as wide as saucers. A low gurgling starts in her throat. Then she jumps up and dashes to the bathroom and slams the door. I hear her retching from the closed door. Gross! I cover my ears and hum to drown it out.

She finally comes out holding a towel, her feet shuffling back to the table. If she'd been healthy, she would be screeching at me by now. All she can manage to say as she glares at me is, "You've got to be messing with me."

"No, Mom, he's on his way over now. He's going to meet up with Dad tomorrow."

Her eyes glaze over and she stares at me uncomprehendingly. "What?" she squeaks.

That's when it hits me; I really have messed up big time. I gulp in some air, trying to backtrack. "Well, uh, while you were at work, Mr. Hanover checked his latest issue of the Central Ohio Musicians Directory, and Dad was listed in it. Everything is there: email, home address and a cell phone number. He's back, Mom."

She shakes her head in denial. Her lips form the word *no*, but nothing comes out. She keeps staring as if I'm speaking a foreign language.

Finally she starts crying hard, choking sobs escaping from her like fireworks exploding on the Fourth of July. I run over and throw my arms around her, telling her it will all be okay.

Chapter Twenty-Three

THE DOORBELL SHRILLS and she cries even harder. I go and let Mike in. He comes hesitantly into the kitchen and sees her wailing away. "Good lord, Angelica!" He turns to me accusingly. "Amber, what's going on?"

I look guilty because I am. I shrug and say, "Mom didn't know we located Dad. There was no time to prepare her. She came home from work sick and went to bed straight away." He looks horrified and then turns from me to Mom.

"Angelica, I am so sorry." He crosses the little room to kneel next to her. He takes one of her hands in his and gently soothes her until she can compose herself. She lifts a puffy face to peek at him.

"Mike, is this for real? Did you actually find Thomas?"

"It's for real, Angelica. It's all true." He throws me an exasperated look. "I am so sorry you were not told this news ahead of time. I know it has to be a great shock."

He throws me another look that lets me know how much he is disappointed in me. I flush and look away. There's nothing I can do or say now that can make up for blabbing. I didn't mean to; it just came up like Old Faithful.

Mike is patting Mom's shoulder but facing my way. She has her head back down on the table, starting to sniffle again.

"Amber, you made me come out tonight because you refused to stick to the agreement we had, which was to wait for me to see how your dad is doing. I don't know what has possessed him to hide from his family and me all these years, but now that he's back, I don't want to overwhelm him or scare him off again. I fear this is exactly what will happen if you insist on being so headstrong."

In reply, I send him a stony look and cross my arms in front of me. He sighs and shakes his head at me.

Mom picks up her head and swivels it from Mike to me again. She's still in a daze.

Mike glances down at her and then gives me a stern look. "Your mom needs time to come to terms with this too. Have a little pity on both your parents."

I stiffen. "What pity has he ever shown me, or for that matter, my mom? I want to know what he's been telling himself all these years, not even sending a letter or a single clue about what he's been up to or where he has been. There's no excuse for it. He made my mom give up trying to figure it all out, and you too, I might add."

Now it is Mike's turn to look embarrassed.

"On top of everything, she's lied about him, whenever I would ask what happened. Talk about some crummy parenting.

I have to deal with these secrets both my parents have had going on for as long as I've been on this planet!" I feel mad and quite justified in continuing my rant until I run out of breath.

Mike looks over at my mom, now sobbing softly, and then narrows his eyes at me. "Are you finished? This is not a perfect world, Amber, and it never has been. You take the good with the bad and try to make the best of things. The world doesn't owe us anything, you know. I understand your frustrations, but things are the way they are, and you learn to roll with whatever comes your way."

I roll my eyes instead. Like I haven't been rolling with the punches from day one, right?

Mom lifts her head straightens her spine and says, "We can count on Mike to tell us everything he finds out after he gets back from seeing your dad, Amber. Mike has always been trustworthy. He did everything possible to help find your dad when he first went missing."

I let out a huge built-up sigh as I look from one adult to the other. I know when I'm beaten, at least temporarily. The two have joined forces, for now.

Mom pulls herself up from her chair and says she needs to go back to bed and rest if there's a chance she will try to work tomorrow.

"Thanks for coming all the way out here, Mike. If I was in better shape, I could offer you some coffee and catch up on old times, but I would not make good company tonight. I bet I look a fright," she adds ruefully, shaking her head.

"It's fine, Angelica, really. Time has not changed your beauty a bit," he says with a little bow and a sad smile. She sends me a sad look and blows a kiss to both of us. Then she shuffles out of the room.

Okay, I feel like barfing now! Got to keep him on my side, though, since he looked so put out with me initially. Plus, he really has come through for us, setting up this meeting with Dad and all.

Mike has been watching my reactions; I am an open book, as the saying goes. He shrugs and looks sad too.

"Amber, I will be in touch sometime tomorrow evening. Weather-wise, things are not looking so great for traveling and the roads out to Logan are bound to be bad. I will do the best I can, but there may be delays or even white-out conditions on the highway because of the crosswinds."

Having said the worst-case scenario, he now tries to give me an encouraging nod as he walks out into the inky night.

Chapter Twenty-Four

JUST SHY OF midnight I put myself to bed, covering my ears as I pass Mom's bedroom due to a cacophony of snores coming through the closed door. With her inability to breathe through a stuffed-up nose, her snoring has reached epic proportions. I try sleeping through the noise by putting my pillow over my head, with no luck. I doubt I could have slept anyway thinking about what my dad will be discussing with Mike. My thoughts are chasing themselves like dogs running after their own tails, so I don't fall asleep until around three in the morning.

IT'S NOW 6:30 and Mom's hacking cough is waking me up. I look out at the white stuff coming down in gobs of fluff and think of the drive ahead for Mike.

Tomorrow is Christmas Eve, and the weather is expected to continue to be snowy and blowy. I see plenty of snow-laden branches creating the all-important Christmas card effect for good little boys and girls. What about for a not-so-perfect teenager like me? And will Mom feel better by then?

How about my dad? Will we find him standing there smiling, stomping his feet to brush off the snow outside our front door, presents in hand for Mom and me? A happy ending like this would be the best Christmas I can ever hope for. But somehow, deep down, I know that is not going to happen. I would be happy for one phone call at this point. I look up at my ceiling, but see past it into the cold, overcast sky above the roof. Are there any Christmas angels like Clarence in the movie *It's A Wonderful Life*? Do you need to earn your wings? Now would be a great time, I plead. I sigh and turn back to reality.

I hear the shower going. Wow, she's going to try and work. I know we need the money, but I am going to talk her out of it. You can't in good conscience bring germs into a nursing home. Maybe some places will look the other way, but those old people don't have enough immunity left to fight off stuff like that. Never mind that's probably where she picked it up in the first place. Turns out that nursing homes are as bad as daycares when it comes to spreading germs around.

I make my short way down to the bathroom and pound on the door. She opens it, bleary-eyed and red-nosed with wet hair. "What? Can't you wait a minute?" she croaks.

"Mom, you're crazy," I say with my hands on my hips. "You know better than to try and work when you're so sick. If they have any sense, they will send you packing anyway." I see the protest forming and hold my hand up. "Don't say it, just dry your hair and go back to bed. I will make cocoa and toast. Call in and say you won't make it in today."

Mom bites her lip, uncertain. I push my point home. "You know I am right. They can survive one day without you."

Her shoulders sag and she shivers in her towel. "I suppose you have a point." She nods and goes back in to dry her hair.

True to my word, I go downstairs and start making toast and cocoa. She will mostly likely rest on the couch after breakfast, which leaves me to do who knows what. Chloe's aunts, uncles and cousins are arriving to stay over for Christmas, so there's no way I want to intrude on their family fun. I text her to wish her a Merry Christmas and say I will try not to bug her until after Christmas about my problems. Chloe texts me and tells me not to be silly and to keep her posted if Mike talks to my dad. Then she wishes me a Merry Christmas.

The toast pops up and I put it on a plate for Mom. She's coming slowly downstairs and joins me at the table.

"There's jam and butter, but I can make you some eggs if you feel like it." I put the cocoa next to her and she tries to smile her thanks.

"Toast is plenty right now, sweetie."

I slide into my seat and look her over. "You need to go back to bed after breakfast." I look at the snow still coming down hard. "Maybe I should call Mike and tell him not to try to be on the road in this weather." I glance her way to gauge her mood. Her eyebrows furl together.

"He's a grown man," she croaks. "He doesn't need your permission to go or not to go." She looks out at the snow. "I think he would be crazy to try it, though," she mutters. "I bet he has a girlfriend or wife who will have something to say about him driving in such awful weather."

I stare at her in surprise. "Do you think so?"

She laughs a phlegmy laugh. "He's my age, so yes, I think he does. And most girlfriends and wives will not look kindly on their loved ones driving unexpectedly way far out somewhere in this mess. Don't be surprised if you get a text saying he has thought better of this expedition." She slurps up the last of her cocoa. "I guess I will go back to bed. Sorry I am such rotten company two days before Christmas. I promise to be better tomorrow." She gets up and shuffles to the refrigerator and takes some meat out of the freezer. "This is filet mignon. The good stuff. I'll let it defrost in the fridge and we can have it with cheesy potatoes and a big salad for Christmas Eve dinner tomorrow." She shows it to me. I see two small round portions of meat, each wrapped with bacon. I wrinkle my nose. "Trust me," she says, "it really is yummy. We can have tiramisu for dessert. I know you like that at least. On Christmas Day we can have lobster tails and homemade mac and cheese and veggies. That is, you will, and I will try to keep my toast and cocoa in my tummy where it belongs!"

She brushes my hair back behind my ears and gives me a pinch on the cheek. She's done that for years, but I wish she wouldn't. I let out a resigned sigh as I hear her footsteps going back upstairs.

Chapter Twenty-Five

I HEAR THE door shut and get up to clear the table. I am putting the jam and butter back when my phone starts buzzing on the table. I have forgotten to turn the sound on after last night. I'm in no hurry to pick it up, since I figure it's Mike calling off the trip out to see Dad. I make myself look at the caller ID and find it is an unknown number. Weird. No one has my number except Chloe, Mom of course, and just a few others.

"Hello?"

A man's deep baritone voice calls my name after a few moments of dead air.

"Amber? Is this Amber?" The voice sounds hesitant yet emotional at the same time.

I suck in my breath—could it possibly be my dad?

"Dad?" I whisper. "Is that you?"

A few seconds of dead air passes between us before the answer comes.

"It's me, Amber, it's your father. I told Mike not to come out today and he gave me your number." His voice is shaky and he's breathing like he's on the verge of hyperventilating.

"Dad!" I sob into the phone. "Oh, Dad, is it you for real?" I can hear him sobbing too. Now he is saying something I cannot comprehend, so I make him repeat himself.

"Amber," he sobs. "You need to forget I exist. We can't do this, sweetie, I'm sorry. Just forget me; you deserve a better father than I can ever be."

I see red, literally. "No!" I shriek. "Don't you dare say that to me, ever! Do you hear me? You owe Mom and me an explanation! I will make Mike bring me to see you and you better not chicken out! You have some nerve not paying child support to Mom all these years. What kind of a father does that? Never mind just walking away from both of us, without any explanation whatsoever. Do you know what you have done to me? I want a dad that will act like a dad. What's wrong with that?"

He says nothing for so long, I wonder if he has already hung up on me. Finally he speaks up. "Nothing, Amber, nothing is wrong with what you want. But I can't give that to you; I wish I could make you understand that I can't be the kind of father you need and should have."

Mom is up and stumbling down the stairs to reach me, almost falling. She squeaks my name hoarsely, demanding to know what's happening. She reaches me, breathless, asking whom I am talking to.

"It's my deadbeat dad, that's who!" I wail, and then yell into my cell again. "You better get yourself over here and tell us

126

the whole story. Tomorrow is Christmas Eve and I want to see you on our front step, got it? No excuses either."

Mom's in shock and is slow to follow the conversation. "Thomas?" she asks in a dazed voice. "Is that you, Thomas?"

He hears her voice and says her name over and over in tortured tones, saying how sorry he is. As she remains speechless, he replies to my demand. "Amber, I am going to FaceTime you so you will understand why I cannot do what you want."

Chapter Twenty-Six

I WAIT FOR the sound alert and then click to connect, still boiling mad. Movement comes across the screen and I stare at it, frowning. A dark-haired man with a mustache and full beard streaked with white appears in the right-hand corner, coming into focus. Then he pushes his phone backward so we can both see he is sitting in a wheelchair. He's missing part of one leg and he stares back at both of us with a pained and ashamed expression.

Mom looks at it, horrified. "Thomas, what happened to you?"

"Oh, Angel, I never wanted you to see me like this. I was so wound up the day we were supposed to meet at our special spot that I didn't time the traffic right. I was jaywalking, sprinting across the road to be super early and arrive first. I wanted everything to be just so—the right table, an open bottle of our favorite wine, even getting Mario to play our favorite song—but it all went wrong. The car hit me and flipped me over it. They said my leg was crushed and I had broken my back. I came to in the hospital and they told me they had to amputate my leg below the knee. That I'd need months for my back to heal and a couple of years of rehabilitation before I could walk with my prosthesis or be on my own. I could think of no reason to drag you into my nightmare, so I let you think I had never bothered to show up at all. I wasn't about to let Mike know of my situation either. I didn't want any awkward pity from him or anyone else."

Mom looks as if she might keel over any second. "We only checked the hospitals in and around Columbus for any word of accidents. We never once thought to check the Cincinnati hospitals. And all this time..." She let her voice trail off.

Dad just nods sadly and then continues to explain. "With no health insurance and unable to work for so long, I ended up homeless for a while. I was too much of a coward, and a prideful one at that, to admit I needed help from anyone." His pleading eyes seek me out. "I am sorry for not paying child support, Amber. I just didn't have it to give. Now that I am finally working part-time again, I can start sending you some of what I owe you and your mom. Please try and forgive me, both of you, if you can."

Now, I am the dumbfounded one. Mom is crying softly, and I find tears streaming down my face too. My breath is coming in gulps. I need to get control or I might pass out. I have been so angry for so long, it's hard not to be the angry me I have been for months on end. Mike sure has it right; life is far from fair.

But here we are, all facing each other at last. The impossible has happened, and today is all unfolding like a play on a stage. I have to do something or say something to hold it to-gether. So being me, I make a quick decision.

"You have no right to bow out of my life again. That is not your choice to make, now that I finally found you again. Mom may or may not want anything to do with you, that remains to be seen. But I want you and you owe it to me to try and have a relationship with your only child. And you need to promise not to disappear again either. So, if you think you can't drive your-self over here, then either Mom or Mike can go out and bring you here, home for Christmas."

Dad covers his face with one hand; his shoulders shake from pent-up emotion. "I feel so ashamed." He slumps back into the wheelchair, a broken man.

"You have been more prideful than cowardly," Mom pro-claims. "That was always your problem. You would never let me get close enough to be a support for you, as I wanted to. You'd shut me out and never discuss what was bothering you." She wipes tears off her face. "I tried to forget you, Thomas, but could never quite manage it. You showed up in my dreams for years. You didn't allow me closure, and that is not fair!" Mom's eyes are flashing now.

I chime in, "And he was about ready to do that again, when he told me I was supposed to just forget about him."

He bows his head, acknowledging this truth. "I have been so lost without you both." He sighs heavily. "I don't have a driver's license anymore and have no money to buy a special-ly equipped car. Some kind neighbors have been taking turns driving me to the bars and pubs I play at on and off. Just so you know, Amber, it will be a long and rocky road to get back to normal, maybe for years to come."

My eyebrows shoot up high. "Yeah? Well, what's normal anyway?" I snort loudly. "There are all types of families out there, and I bet they all face their own set of challenges."

Now that I have said that, a picture of Chloe and her perfect family pops into my head from nowhere. From the outside looking in, it has always appeared perfect. But now it dawns on me, there is no such thing as a perfect family, including Chloe's. My eyes start watering and I feel bad because I have never bothered to ask her if there was anything I could do for her, not in all the years we have been friends. Being selfish doesn't come close to describing how I have acted towards her. I shake my head to clear it. I have to focus on my family in the here and now. But I know I have some apologizing of my own to do later.

I turn to Mom. "We can get him, right? Get Dad here and spend Christmas Eve and Christmas together?" I wait for her answer, filled with triumph.

Chapter Twenty-Seven

I FUME WHEN I see both parents shaking their heads simultaneously.

"Amber, I know how badly you want this to happen, but I cannot in good conscience get way out to Logan, in this awful weather, with roads in such terrible shape."

Dad backs her up. "Your mother is right, Amber. I would never be able to forgive myself if something were to happen to either of you, because of me."

I scrunch up my face, getting ready to explode.

"Amber, we can call your dad tomorrow and decide if Christmas Day would be better on the roads. We can FaceTime both tomorrow and on Christmas if the weather doesn't allow us to drive out there and get him. Try and be satisfied with that for now."

I see both determination and that stubborn look she gets when she makes up her mind. It doesn't slow me down a bit.

"You'll see. The weather will turn around and we can get Dad over, at least for Christmas Day." I'm guessing I can be as stubborn as the two of them combined.

They both crack smiles again and I start to relax. "We will do our best," Mom promises.

"Well, I better sign off for now," Dad says. "My physical therapist is coming soon to work with me. Rotten weather or not, he always shows up. Good thing he doesn't have to drive far in this blizzard. I have been slacking off lately and he hasn't been happy with me. Wait till I tell him I have a real reason to push through all the hard exercises he makes me do. I really have something to look forward to now, and it's all due to you, Amber."

Then he looks shyly towards Mom. "I am grateful you are even talking to me, Angelica. There are no words I can say to express how sorry I am for all the pain I have caused you. I don't expect you to forgive me." He looks overwhelmed with sadness again.

"We will talk tomorrow, Thomas." She looks drained of energy. "I will do my best to put the past behind us. We will see where tomorrow will take us, but I can't make any promises about anything. I do know that Amber needs you in her life and I would never do anything to keep her from you. You need each other."

Hey, that's a start anyhow. I beam at both of them. They smile shyly at each other again and say goodbye.

Chapter Twenty-Eight

THE SCREEN GOES dark. I turn and hug Mom. "Thanks," I say. "You look beat, Mom. You better go back upstairs and take a nap."

"I think I will," she says and pulls herself to a standing position, but still leans on the chair. "I can hardly believe this all just happened. I might need you to pinch me to be sure I am awake."

I laugh. "You are awake, but you need to go back to sleep." I turn her around and walk her to the doorway. "Can you climb the stairs without any help?"

"Amber, I work at a nursing home, but it doesn't mean I need to live in one yet!" She manages a teasing voice, so I won't worry so much.

"Okay, get some winks and I will check in on you later. I want to tell Chloe that Dad called."

Mom turns around at the top of the stairs and gives me a troubled look. "Don't take up too much of her time on the phone. Carol probably needs her help with the little nieces and nephews."

"I know, I know; I promise." She closes her door. Instantly, I am texting Chloe about Dad's call. I hope she will answer; yeah, I'm back to being selfish, I know. I hit send and stare at my cell. No reply. I frown and put it down. I wander idly over to the TV and start looking through our ancient DVD collection yet again.

My phone rings and I grab it up. Chloe is calling, not texting. "Hey!" I answer. "Did you get my…"

I need not have asked because she squeals in my ear. "OMG, Amber! He called you? This is beyond awesome! Tell me everything he said and don't leave anything out."

And so I do, talking nonstop for the next half hour.

Chapter Twenty-Nine

CHRISTMAS EVE dawns with weak sunlight bravely trying to find a crack through the clouds. I roll out of bed and make my way down the hall, to be the first one to shower. I have a lot on my mind as to what to give Dad for a Christmas present. I decide, as I run hot water in the tiny shower, which quickly fogs up, that I will draw a picture of Dad and myself next to him. A father-daughter portrait will be the best present I can think of. I won't put Mom in, since I am not sure where their relationship is headed.

By the time I am out of the bathroom, Mom is chomping at the bit to get in. She tells me Mike and his girlfriend are coming over later for a short visit before they go to eat Christmas Eve dinner. She says she feels up to having them over. I shrug and say okay.

I pad barefoot down the hall to get dressed, but I am not sure what to wear or how dressed up I should be to meet Mike's girlfriend. I throw all my clothes around looking for something nice, but not too nice. That shouldn't be hard, because I never get that dressed up to begin with. I know that plaid shirts are coming back in style and jeans have never gone out. But I opt for leggings and a lacy top, which is as fancy as I get.

Mom is out of the shower and we pass each other in the hall. I know she is somewhat better, because in typical mom fashion, she wrinkles her nose up and shakes her head at me. "You are going to freeze in that outfit," she warns.

I respond with my typical eye roll and tell her it's my choice. She shrugs and goes to get dressed. I make my way downstairs, pop in a bagel, and grab some orange juice while eyeing the weather anxiously. Sunbeams are breaking through the clouds, but we're still getting flurries. I can hear Mom already in my head telling me the roads won't be ready for the trip out to Logan.

Mom comes down and makes coffee for herself. She digs out a recipe for the filet mignon we will be having tonight and then goes to get it out of the fridge to get it up to room temperature because they are still half frozen. She mumbles to herself about not overcooking it as she reads through the recipe.

"Do you want rare or medium rare, when I start cooking them later on?"

"You know I have never had them before, so how do I know?" I frown. "Are they steaks? They look pretty small. What else will we have?"

"Oh, scalloped potatoes, I guess, and maybe broccoli or Brussels sprouts with bacon bits. I can mix them with bacon grease and they will be real tasty that way." I nod, okay with either one.

"What's Dad going to eat?" I ask, even though I know he will not be able to join us. She confirms this by shaking her head and turning on the weather channel, so I can't fight her on her decision. I hear the weather guy yammering on about how bad the roads are the further out you go past central Ohio. Icy road conditions and a level two emergency are in effect for Hocking County, where Dad is.

I ball up my fists, feeling more frustrated than I have felt for some time. "This totally sucks!" I say vehemently.

She shoots me a sympathetic look, but with no comment, and continues to put out the ingredients for seasoning the meat.

"Remember, Mike and Sheila will stop by around three o'clock before they go downtown. They are dining out at Cap City Diner at six and then on to a party with some friends."

"Goody for them," I grump. "I'm going upstairs to make a Christmas present for Dad. And you better tell him we will pick him up tomorrow, no matter what the roads look like."

With that I leave her in a huff without cleaning up my mess from breakfast and without any protest, I might add, from my mother.

I get busy sharpening my colored pencils and finding some big paper with a little tooth to it. Next, I take some computer paper to do a thumbnail sketch for a preliminary composition. I decide on backlighting, which will cause a little halo around both of us against a dark background, for a dramatic effect. I start to sketch, pursing my lips like I am sucking on a lemon. It takes me forty minutes just to get the pose right and to adjust the likeness of my dad, which makes him look older than I had originally pictured him to be. Fact is: he *is* older and a lot less carefree, obviously, than he was in his younger years before the accident.

I close my eyes and picture his face from yesterday. His brow is deeply marked with a set of permanent lines and his cheeks are thin and chiseled, not as filled out as in his younger years. His hair is shot through with gray. Hard times can age one fast, I think.

But nothing has changed his beaming smile. That remains a thousand-kilowatt glow, proving that he still can enjoy life, no matter what it throws at him. Now that I am satisfied with the initial sketch, I grid it up into squares with a ruler and double the size measurements for the final portrait. I slowly draw the features square by square to keep the proportions accurate. Another forty minutes goes by and then I decide I need a break before I start the color penciling, which will take forever. I go down to the kitchen to find a snack and get a drink.

The vacuum is going in the living room; she is trying to clean up before Mike and his girlfriend get here. Mom spots me and asks if I can dust a little. I shrug and say sure, in a few minutes. She leaves off vacuuming and heads down to clean the powder room.

I stick my head in the refrigerator to find something to nibble on and notice the meat still sitting out. I sigh and put it back in the fridge; even *I* know you shouldn't leave uncooked meat, especially chicken, out that long. I sigh as I pull out some grapes and flavored fizzy water. I'd rather have a pop, but Mom thinks we need to start eating healthier. Chloe and her mom must be rubbing off on her.

Thinking of Chloe, I wish I could call or at least text her, but she needs some family time and I realize I would appear too needy. I sigh again and hunt up a dust rag. I wander into the living room and start half-heartedly swiping at the coffee table, and then the end table and computer desk. How much dust can there be in the winter anyway?

Then it hits me; why not call Dad? What a concept! I can actually pick up my cell and call my dad now. Better yet, I will FaceTime him.

I call out that I am getting ahold of him on my cell. Mom comes to stand inside the doorway with a look of surprise, holding the toilet cleaner in her rubber-gloved hands.

"Do you think it's okay? What if he's taking a nap or something?"

I say scornfully, "What—in the middle of the morning? Don't be silly." I key in his number and hit FaceTime. It rings and rings at first, then gets connected.

I see a beaming face in the upper right-hand corner.

"Hi, Amber, honey. How are you today?"

"How's it going, Dad? Just checking in on you and getting some idea of when we can pick you up tomorrow for Christmas. I can't wait to see you."

Worry clouds his face. "The roads here are still on a level two emergency. What does your mom think?"

She is hastily stripping off the rubber gloves and setting the toilet cleaner on the end table. "Road conditions here are improving some, now that the snow has stopped," she reports. She gets closer to my phone, so she can get a view of Dad too. "We should keep close tabs on the weather report for your neck of the woods, Thomas. I mean, I want to be able to come get you, but we have to be wise." She sends a sideways glance at me and sees my face turning red and my mouth opening and shutting fast. I am ready to explode.

"I agree, Angelica. It's better to be safe than sorry."

"Dad!" I protest sharply, but he cuts me off.

"I know, Amber, really, I know. I will be terribly disappointed too. Let's take it one step at a time. Snow warriors will be working through the night here to try to make the roads safe enough to travel for tomorrow. They all realize how important a day it is for so many folks, and they will do their best. That's all we can hope for. If worse comes to worst, we will wish each other Merry Christmas using FaceTime. Just be glad we have such amazing technology to connect. Your mom and I sure didn't!"

"But I want you here," I wail like a two-year-old. Tears come out of nowhere. "I want to give you your Christmas present in person; I've been working on it all morning."

"Sweetie!" He takes a deep breath. "Just being able to talk to you and see your face now is the best Christmas present I could ever wish for."

I sniff and reach out for the tissue Mom is holding out to me. Then I square my shoulders and stand taller.

"I am not ready to give up on actually standing in your doorway to bring you back home for Christmas. I will deliver your present directly into your hands. That's my new Christmas wish and I am not giving it up!"

Mom and Dad are both smiling tolerantly. "Well, remember to wish on a star tonight, baby," says Dad.

"Then we will just have to leave it up to Mother Nature and Providence to provide a good outcome," Mom chimes in. They smile at each other, once more a united front.

"Well, I should probably get back to my exercises I promised my therapist I would work on. I want to be in good shape and keep up with all your activities, Amber, when we get together." He winks at Mom. "I know your mom was an athlete all through school, but don't wear her out too much before I can see you both. Fingers crossed for tomorrow and much love to you…both," he adds as his face vanishes from the screen.

Mom stares at the blank screen for a second more and then murmurs, "It is all so like a dream; I can still hardly take it in." Then she snaps out of it and says, "Okay, I better get back to straightening the upstairs now, and make my bed and all. It would be nice for you to make your bed too, Amber."

I grimace and whine, "What the heck for? Nobody is going upstairs anyhow."

Hands on her hips, she says, "That is not the point. We don't need to be sloppy. How many times have you asked me where this or that got to, only to find it later, under a pile of stuff you didn't put away? Stay neat and pick it up the first time around. It makes you feel better too, when everything is in its place and put away. It feels good to live in a clean home."

I make blah, blah motions with my hand and she gives me a cagey look. "Besides, Amber, we want everything tidied up and looking nice for your dad now, don't we?"

That argument turns me around without further resistance and sends me upstairs to tidy up my room. After I am done, I realize she tricked me. How would he get upstairs anyhow? He's in a wheelchair and not too handy with using his prosthesis, so no upstairs for him any time soon.

I shrug off the neat way she tricked me and sit behind my desk to start coloring in my dad and me. No getting around it, this will take hours of patiently building up colors, blending layer by layer to achieve the perfect skin tones and hair color. I give it my all and barely move for the next few hours, until I hear the loud knocking on the front door and realize that Mike and Sheila have arrived.

Chapter Thirty

"MIKE, IT'S SO good to see you and it's good of you to come out in this frigid weather. Let me take your coats." And then she calls me as I am on my way down. Like our place is so huge she can't see me coming. She's funny like that.

"Hi Mike," I say and then shake hands with Sheila. She is a short, rail-thin blond lady with a starved model look about her. Why do guys always go for this type? She smiles, but not a big smile, like she's afraid she'll crack her face or something. They are both dressed up for dinner later on. Mom waves them over to the couch. They sit side by side on the edge, like they are afraid to wrinkle their good clothes. Talk about awkward!

Mom offers hot tea, cocoa, or coffee and they both ask for herbal tea. I tell her I will heat up the water in the microwave and pop the tea bags in, which makes Sheila wrinkle her nose up a bit. I am left to wonder if I've prepared the tea improperly. I bring back cookies and crumb cake that Mom left on the kitchen table. Mike selects crumb cake, but Sheila declines both. I take a cookie and start crunching. Mike asks Mom how she is feeling, and she says better and better, now that we talked to Dad again today.

As I bring in the tea, Mom jovially asks them where they both met. Sheila starts talking and then I get it. She has a British accent so that must make her an expert on the afternoon tea-time and quite an interesting person to an American guy from Ohio. He puts his arm around her and grins as she relates how they met at a club in downtown Columbus when she was on vacation from the Cotswolds, where she lives in England.

Mike had been playing jazz trombone that night and so the rest was history. They have had a long-distance relationship for the past several years, which has become more permanent since Sheila's company, which sells antique and vintage jewelry, sent her to the US to do business with vintage jewelry stores here in Columbus. I try and stifle a yawn at their long-winded tale.

Finally, Mike gets around to quizzing Mom about how she feels about picking up my dad tomorrow for Christmas.

"We are both keeping tabs on the level two emergency travel advisory. I told Thomas if it is still this way tomorrow, we might have to hold off until after Christmas to see him in person. There may be a little hope that the roads will be kept plowed and salted enough to get out there, but I am not holding my breath and neither is he. Thomas says he quite understands and wants us both to stay safe."

Both Mike and Sheila notice my obvious downcast expression. It seems Sheila has been brought up to speed by Mike about our family situation because she clucks sympathetically.

"I hear you are a very determined young lady, judging by how you located your dad with Mike's help," she says in her crisp and clipped British accent. "I do admire your persistent efforts to bring him home and I hope everything turns out for the best for you both." Her smile now takes in my mom as well. I begin to think my opinion of her was formed a little too quickly.

That's the problem with meeting someone for the first time. First impressions can be deceiving, and I feel guilty for having jumped to conclusions about her. I should know, because apparently, I don't always give off such good first impression vibes myself. But then, kids at school rarely give someone a second chance, due to the constant gossiping and so-called reputations.

I hope that after winter break the grapevine will be relaying a different kind of story about me after I make it clear that my dad is alive after all and that he is back in my life permanently.

The thought brings a hopeful smile to my lips, which the grown-ups believe is a result of Sheila's encouragement. Their visit comes to a close and we all stand up and wish each other Merry Christmas. I throw in a Happy New Year for good measure. Mom hands their coats to them and sees them to the door. We all wave our goodbyes and shut the door on the cold outside. I find myself still shivering for a full five minutes after they leave, and it is not due to the cold. My emotions are gearing up for the next main event—being with Dad, all of us together for Christmas.

Chapter Thirty-One

"WELL, THAT WAS a very nice time," Mom repeats as if to comfort herself that all went well in the grand scheme of things. "I think I need a nap before I clean up around here and then start our special menu for tonight." She eyes me and asks, "You sure have been busy up in your room all day. What's going on up there?"

"I told you already, I am working on Dad's present. It is a portrait of the two of us together. I hope he will like it." I start fretting that maybe it's not turning out as great as I'd hoped.

"Amber, what a fantastic idea! I can't wait to see it, and I know your dad will be thrilled." Her praise, even though she has yet to see it, perks me up. That's a mom for you; they can give a boost to your ego, if they stop nagging at you long enough to do it!

"I'm going back up to put on the finishing touches," I announce. "Be down later to help set the table." I watch her finish loading the dishes in the dishwasher and putting the snack munchies away in the closet. I should help, but I am already picturing what needs to be changed on my portrait.

I head for the stairs as she looks for a dishrag to wipe up some crumbs on the coffee table. I remind her to get a nap in and stop worrying about crumbs.

Back at my desk, I apply a critical eye to my work. The halo behind our heads is glowing a little too brightly, so I dial that effect back a little. We aren't angels in heaven, after all! We haven't been a family for ten years, and even when they were married, it wasn't all sweetness and light. But there was love once, and if we all spent some time together, there might be a chance of having Dad in our house again. One corner of my mind still remains pessimistic and hears warning bells going off, while the other half stays stubbornly optimistic.

Now I check the smiles. Dad's looks spot on, but mine looks a bit toothy. Teeth are the hardest things to get right in portraits. I wish people wouldn't smile so much, but they insist on showing the world that their lives are perfect and that they haven't got a care anywhere within a ten-mile radius. As if!

I decide to give the most attention to getting the first four upper teeth right, and then I will create an impression of the rest of them in the mouth. After I work for awhile, I tilt my head to assess what I have done and feel good about it. I add more shading and even out all the skin tones. This takes up the better part of the late afternoon, until I notice how dark it's getting.

I glance at the time; it is almost five o 'clock. Yes, it's pitch black out. Right on cue, I hear Mom calling me to get downstairs and give her a hand with dinner. I will have to spray fixative on the colored pencil later, so it won't smudge before taking the long drive out to Dad's for Christmas Day. I can't believe I'll be seeing him tomorrow. I feel an electric shock going through me at this thought.

I had always imagined him showing up on our doorstep, but now we will be showing up on his, instead. Life's funny that way. Not to worry, though. I send a little look upward. "You did good work here, Clarence," I whisper. "Everything is going to be just fine. Not perfect, but just fine!"

Chapter Thirty-Two

MOM AND I have a good dinner, without having to go out to some loud and crowded restaurant where you get stuck waiting for hours. Her filet mignon turned out pretty good—I have mine medium well and she has hers medium rare, to be kind to her stomach. She tells me she really likes it rare.

"Got to live a little on the wild side, every now and then." She grins, stretching out her legs and leaning back in her chair. "Your dad and I had a blast in high school. He loved sports of all kinds, especially pole vaulting." She is in a chatty mood, reminiscing about good times with Dad. That isn't all bad.

"Dad said you were an athlete too. You never told me that."

"You never asked." She laughs, shaking her head. "I ran track. I got awards in the 800-meter races at two hours and fifty minutes, sometimes less if I pushed myself. While training, I tried running thirty to forty miles a week."

"Impressive!" And I am impressed. My mother was a star athlete; who would have guessed? Then her face clouds up. "Your dad probably will not want to look back on those days, Amber. Not after what's happened to him. Best not to bring that sort of memory up, if we see him tomorrow."

"You mean when, right? When we see him. Besides, he's the one who mentioned athletics; he must have been very proud of your achievements."

"We had a lot in common back then. Now probably not so much." She gets up to clear dishes.

I get up too and help her. "Well, you have one extremely important thing in common: yours truly! So start there and look for more subjects of good conversation. That's what you always tell me when I say people are a pain in the you-know-what."

Now she takes a turn at rolling her eyes. Ha! I could remind her where I picked up that habit, but I won't.

I change the subject instead. "Let's listen to the latest weather report, so we can figure out the best time to leave in the morning."

So we turn on the weather channel for the fourth time today and see that things are turning around some. The level two near Dad has been reduced to a level one. I do a fist pump and let out a whoop. Mom still looks doubtful, but I ignore her and hop around the room in excitement.

"What time can we get going in the morning?"

"Probably around ten o'clock, if roads are safe enough. I will call your dad and see what he thinks in the morning." She wraps up the leftovers and starts digging in the fridge for extra food we could take to Dad's. "There's some leftover ham and turkey to make sandwiches. Not what one would call anything close to a Christmas feast, but better than nothing? We will put whatever we can into the cooler and take it to him. Maybe some Bob Evans will be open part of the day and we can pick up turkey and gravy." She murmurs, talking to herself again, which is how she rolls.

After placing the wrapped-up food into Tupperware for tomorrow, she smiles and says it's time for me to open presents. She goes into the mudroom and opens the cabinets over the washer and dryer. She pulls out some wrapped gifts and brings them to me. I grin and start tearing into them. As expected, much of it turns out to be clothes that I will have to wait to wear until next spring. She did manage to pick out some cool pierced earrings and a gold necklace. And as always, she bought me more art supplies, which I always welcome.

I thank her and say, "Hold the phone!" I dash up to my room to find the presents I got for her, which include a book and new, warm flannel pajamas and soft slippers. She says she will put them on right away and head off to bed, so she will be up to driving to Logan, if the weather cooperates.

I reassure her it will all be fine and follow her upstairs to put the spray fixative on the portrait and pick out something special to wear when I see my dad for the first time in a decade.

I am once again sifting through my wardrobe and not noticing anything more than before. We never go anywhere, so what is the point of buying dressy stuff we can't afford anyway? I start yanking out clothes and throwing them on the bed, as if that will bring something to light. Nothing…no, wait! Way in the back of the closet hangs a dress that I had forgotten about. Chloe actually gave it to me, 'cause Chloe and her mom had gone shopping and bought her new dresses, which she actually gets to do whenever she feels like it. I take it out and eye it appraisingly. It is a faux leather dress with long puffed sleeves and a scooped neck. She only wore it once and then decided it wasn't for her. What was high above the knee on her would come several inches below mine. With my dress boots, it will be fine. Yes! Perfect!

Next, I rummage around in my desk drawer for some tissue paper to wrap around the portrait for my dad, which I sandwich between two pieces of cardboard, to keep it safe. I'm ready for tomorrow.

As I head back downstairs, I can hear snoring from Mom's bedroom. I figure she will keep sleeping the remainder of the evening and on through the night. She needs it. I clean up the rest of the stuff left out and pop the dishes into the dishwasher.

With the cleanup finished, I head off to the living room and turn the TV on low. I start flipping channels and land on the Hallmark channel. The show features some guy and a woman declaring their undying love to each other, after they had been apart for years because of some misunderstanding or other. I watch the remainder of it and as it comes to its inevitable conclusion, I am happier for it. They always have happy endings. Then I climb the stairs up to bed, tuck myself in, and find some soft music to fall asleep to. I want to dream about a snowy white Christmas morning, but one that will have drivable roads, so I will get to see my long-lost father.

Chapter Thirty-Three

I AM UP early Christmas morning, looking anxiously out the window and then rushing down the hall to jump in the shower. Yes, it is snowing, but only a few flakes at a time. They twirl their way down from a sky that is trying to clear up. I am practically dancing on air as I knock loudly on my mom's door, as I go by yelling, "Wake up, Mom, Merry Christmas," before I duck in the shower. I hurry as fast as I can so she can get a turn.

She stands outside the door in her new pajamas, waiting; her nose still bright as a cherry from blowing it constantly. Not as bright-eyed or bushy-tailed as I would like to see, but still up and ready to get herself together.

"Turn on the weather report and see what's going on while I get ready, okay? And maybe make some eggs while you're at it. I'll make bacon when I come down."

She shuts the bathroom door. I hurry to dress, while thinking, *I will do you one better. I will call Dad and see what is going on myself.* I quickly finish getting into the dress and then rush down-stairs, where I left my phone still charging. I call him right up.

"Merry Christmas, Dad!" I shout, when he picks up. "Are you ready for us to come over?" I act like we live down the street, instead of two hours away.

He looks at me a little bleary-eyed, but answers me in a cheery tone, "Well, Merry Christmas to you too, sweetie. How are you and your mom this morning?"

"Everything's great and we can't wait to see you! What's the weather doing there? Mom says we can leave here at ten a.m."

A smile tugs at the corner of his mouth. "Oh, does she? Can you put her on, honey? We need to make sure we are on the same page about everything."

"Oh, she's still in the shower; has the snow stopped?"

Next I hear, "No, actually, I am right behind you, Amber!" And there she is with her hair wrapped in a towel. Now how did she manage that so quickly? "Let me talk to your dad, please, right now." And she takes my phone out of my hand.

"Merry Christmas, Thomas. How are you?" She gazes in-tently into the live feed of him on FaceTime. "What's the weath-er like there and how are the roads?"

"Merry Christmas, Angelica," he says softly. I can tell he is gaga over her, the way his voice sounds and how his eyes cannot leave her face. I can see this happening as I stand next to her. It's obvious to me. Is it to her?

"Weather here is slowly getting back to normal and the level two has dropped to a level one." He reports the facts, but his eyes never leave hers.

"Well, it has pretty much stopped snowing here, so I think we can make the attempt to come on out to you. Are you up to a visit from us, Thomas?" she asks anxiously.

"It would be most welcome and wonderful, if you think you want to try coming out in this weather. Remember, it is entirely up to you; if you feel it isn't safe, then we can wait for a better opportunity." I am hopping up and down from one foot to the other, about ready to burst.

She mulls things over for another few seconds and then replies in the affirmative. "It might take us longer than it normally would to get there, but I think we can give it a try."

"Yes!" I screech and fist pump toward the ceiling.

"But just to be clear, if I think roads are turning too slick, I am turning back, Amber. We need to stay safe." She gives me a warning look.

"Okay, deal!" I say impatiently and turn away to make some breakfast ASAP. I grab the frying pan and rummage for eggs in the fridge.

I hear her repeating the address he gives her, so she can put it into the GPS. She also adds it to her contacts as Dad signs off to get ready for our visit.

"He kind of looks tired out and not terribly healthy to me," she muses to herself as I bustle around cracking the eggs into the pan and letting them cook slow.

She opens the fridge hunting for bacon, but I stop her in her tracks. "Bacon takes too long. I'll put in some toast and here's juice. Let's eat and get out of here."

"Oh, all right. I guess my stomach doesn't need the extra grease this morning anyway." She pours the juice out as I plate up the eggs. I toss a couple of pieces of toast into the toaster and add a little cheese to the eggs, for more a more flavorful taste.

We start munching and the toasts pops up. She gets up and brings it to the table, putting butter and jam next to me.

"So I do not want to tire him or stay too long, Amber, this first time around. He always been one to talk a good talk, but I think he is more fragile than he lets on."

"Okay, Mom, I get it," I say between wolfing bites of egg and toast together. "I need to brush my teeth, then I'll be ready."

She gives a little laugh and looks down at her bathrobe, which she threw on over her PJ's when she heard me on the phone. "I have to make myself presentable first, you know. I will try to be as quick as I can." She takes the towel off her head and goes upstairs to dry her hair and get ready.

I bite my lip impatiently. I should have figured this. They haven't seen each other in a decade, so she is going to take some time with her appearance. I blow a raspberry through my lips and start cleaning up, desperate for something to do besides going cray-cray.

When Mom finally comes downstairs, I have to look twice because she is all made up and doesn't even look like herself. Her hair is curled, her makeup perfect and her dress is a shimmering, silky purple with gathered ruching resting on her hip, adding extra slimming through the waist and side.

"Wow, Mom, you look...amazing!"

She blushes a little and then says thanks. "We really should get going. I actually packed a few extra things for both of us, in case we get stranded by any weather changes or whatnot." She looks thoughtful.

"Fine by me," I say enthusiastically. I wouldn't mind staying there an extra day to see more of Dad.

Mom pulls the food she packed last night out of the fridge and pulls a mid-sized suitcase alongside her.

"Hey, I'll get it. You can put the food in the little cooler and then we will be ready, right?"

We grab our coats, bring everything outside, load it up, and hit the road. Mom is being overly cautious as usual, but I don't say a word. She has to feel good about this or I am afraid she will turn around and head back to the starting gate. No way will I let that happen.

She says she has to stop for gas and buy de-icer. She even put blankets in the back seat and sand in the trunk, in case we get stuck, somehow.

The sun is shining but it is windy and freezing. She checks her tire pressure and then turns on the GPS to head out of town. We are on I-70 E toward Wheeling awhile and then take exit 132 for OH 13. This takes some time and she is gritting her teeth and white-knuckling it already. We finally get to OH 256W and look for OH 664 South.

All this time our tiny old Honda Civic is getting shoved around in the crosswinds. We are taking a beating between the winds, which are blowing up tons of drifting snow across the windshield, and the fact that the roads are mostly glare ice in many spots. Mom is trying to follow the grooves of previous tracks left by other travelers. Right now we are the only ones on the highway.

"You're doing great, Mom, really." I am making an effort at cheerleading, but even I think we might very well land in a ditch and soon.

She is actively grinding her teeth and her death grip on the steering wheel is relentless. "I let you talk me into this, Amber. I am a poor excuse for a mother. Plus, we are dressed like idiots in these dresses when it is icy cold out there. If we run off the road, I don't know what will happen to us! But we have come too far to turn back now."

"It can't be that much farther now," I say, trying to keep the panic out of my voice.

A ways up ahead I spot some blinking blue and white lights as the drifting snow takes a break from blinding us.

"I think that's a snowplow. We can just follow it from now on, Mom!" I say excitedly. She heaves a sigh of relief as we catch up to it.

We get to follow it for a while until we find Walnut Street, and then onto 641 East Front Street where Dad rents an apartment in the building. Fortunately, he has a ground floor unit.

Mom is still shaky and works to unclench her fingers from the steering wheel.

"Thanks to God we got here in one piece!" she says in a trembling voice. She takes her cell phone out of the hands-free holder and dials Dad to announce our arrival. He says he already unlocked his door and to come on in. He says sorry about not helping us bring things in. Mom reassures him not to worry.

We unload the food and I carry my present in a tote.

Mom sees the glare ice on the steps and cautions me about it since I have dress boots on. She is carrying her shoes and has ugly outdoor boots on. Go figure!

I note that there is a cheap wooden ramp off the side of the steps, so I opt for that. I reach the door handle and stop a moment. I know I am holding my breath. I love my dad and I need him in my life. I believe he needs me too. I look over my shoulder at Mom. Her eyes are enormous and wet with tears. She smiles wordlessly and gives me a nod. She needs him too.

I let my breath out slowly, open the door, and go inside.

THE END

About the Author

BETTE MILLAT is the mother of three wonderful grown children. She is a hands-on grandmother of four incredible grandchildren, all of whom keep her young! She has a Bachelor of Fine Arts from the Columbus College of Art and Design, and a Bachelor's Plus in teaching middle school Language Arts and Social Studies. She also holds a master's degree in Education from Ashland University.

Bette has been a teacher and tutor for children in kindergarten through middle school for twenty years. She currently gives painting lessons to adults and children in Ohio, and is the author and illustrator of *Sparkle the Runaway Snowflake*, a children's book published in 2019.